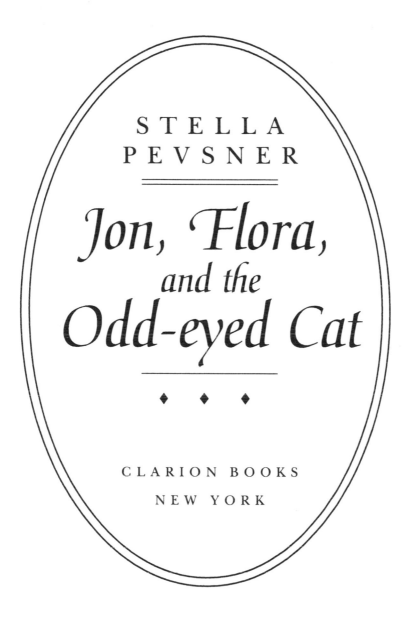

STELLA
PEVSNER

Jon, Flora,
and the
Odd-eyed Cat

◆   ◆   ◆

CLARION BOOKS

NEW YORK

Clarion Books
a Houghton Mifflin Company imprint
215 Park Avenue South, New York, NY 10003
Text copyright © 1994 by Stella Pevsner

Text is 12-point New Baskerville

Printed in the USA

Library of Congress Cataloging-in-Publication Data

Pevsner, Stella.
Jon, Flora, and the odd-eyed cat / by Stella Pevsner.
p. cm.
Summary: While recovering from rheumatic fever and a move
from Chicago to a small southern town, fourteen-year-old Jon
becomes involved with a troubled young girl's recreation of
an ancient druid ceremony.
ISBN 0-395-67021-7
[1. Druids and druidism—Fiction.
2. Rheumatic fever—Fiction.   3. Moving, Household—Fiction.
4. Family problems—Fiction.]   I. Title.
PZ7.P44815Jo   1994
[Fic]—dc20
                                                    93-41218
                                                       CIP
                                                        AC

BP   10   9   8   7   6   5   4   3   2   1

For my wonderful grandson, Laurence
(who may grow up to love cats)

S ometimes it seems that the events of last summer never happened at all. They could have been things conjured up by my fevered mind. And then I go on to wonder if Flora herself was real, or if I imagined her and her strange ways. But then Kat comes around, and he is living evidence. Yes, Kat. Kat is very real.

All in all, it was a summer that broke all the regular patterns of my life. There were so many changes during those three months.

The biggest exterior change was that my family moved to the South. That in itself would have been enough of a jolt to a guy who'd always lived in a Chicago suburb, and always in the same house. But I was also sick at the time, slowly recovering from rheumatic fever.

Rheumatic fever, as you may know, is a lingering, boring kind of illness. It starts with a throat infection and then settles in the joints and heart. I got it sometime in April and had to stay in bed for the last weeks of ninth grade.

"It seems to me, Jon, that your family can't move now," my friend Eddie had said hopefully when he was visiting me one day after school.

"We have to," I'd told him. "Dad's already started his new job down in South Carolina and the house is all set, waiting for us."

"Couldn't they just cancel all that?"

"Sure, Eddie," I'd said, shifting my aching legs on the bed. "Dad should go tell the medical supply company that he's decided to drop the job, and then be unemployed for umpteen years!" Even I could hear the near hysteria in my voice.

"Don't get hyper," Eddie said. "I was just asking."

"Sorry," I muttered. "It's just . . ." I punched up the pillow behind my head. Being sick had not given me a great attitude.

Teresa, my almost-seventeen-year-old sister, had pointed out this fact to me. "Look, Jon, I don't want to move any more than you do," she said. "But I'm trying to be mature about it."

"That's because you're going away to college anyway this fall. That's why it's not such a big deal for you," I told her.

"Then think about Mother," Teresa said. "She's leaving all her friends, too, but you don't hear her whining about it."

"She . . . she wouldn't," I said. It was true. My

mother was not the complaining type. She took flak from all of us and still stayed composed.

I knew she was very concerned about me, though, and so was Dad. He flew up from Leesville whenever he could. On his last visit the doctor was at the house.

"Jon's still so feverish," Dad said. "I'm wondering . . ."

"That'll be with him awhile," Dr. Gordon said. "However, I'd say he can make the move provided he stays in bed now and goes right to bed in the new place and takes it easy all summer."

"All summer!" I yelped.

"Hush, honey," Mom said, adjusting the pillow under my legs. "Do they still ache?"

"No, I feel fine," I said through clenched teeth. Let them all ruin my life and be done with it. I shifted to my side, turning my back on my parents and the doctor.

They all left the room then but I could hear them talking out in the hall. Dad told the doctor he'd already contacted his colleague in Leesville and that Dr. Arlo sounded very competent. Great. There was a conspiracy going to keep me bedridden forever. I knew, even as I thought this, that it was unfair of me, but I was in no mood to be anything but disagreeable.

◆

The move to Leesville wasn't bad. After the furniture went, we stayed with relatives in Chicago for a week and then flew down. I felt okay, but once we got to the new house I was glad to see my bed all set up, and more or less collapsed into it. Those first few days are blurred in my mind. I remember, though, that my legs buckled one day when I tried to get up and walk. Also—and I'm ashamed to say this—I remember that in my groggy state, I slapped at Dad's hand when he tried to feel my forehead.

"Could everyone just leave me alone?" I'd bellowed. Dad didn't deck me. Even if I'd been okay he wouldn't have. Eddie had said a couple of times that my parents were nice beyond belief and I was nothing like them. He was probably right.

At first there was nothing to give shape or form to the drowsy, feverish days as I lay in my bed upstairs, hearing the occasional voices downstairs. I could make out the soft murmur of my mother's voice but not her actual words as she talked to strangers brought in to repair things, to deliver new furniture, or just to help us settle into the new house.

I'd awaken to the morning sun streaming into my room, with leaf shadows on my bed from the tree outside the nearer window. The farther window looked out upon a meadow, and there was a roof just below both windows.

Dad often brought up my breakfast before he left for work in the morning and stayed awhile, talking about sports or things going on in the town. I made a feeble attempt to act interested, because I knew none of this was easy for him, either. I was also aware of him sitting in my room the first few nights, just in case I needed something. He didn't mention it, though, and neither did I.

Teresa would come for my breakfast tray and complain about what a slug I was while she was working her fingers to the bone, helping Mom do closets and cupboards. But I could tell she was concerned about me, too.

During the long afternoons I would read until the inevitable headache took over. Then I'd lie there, listening to the soft whir of the fan on the hardwood floor, and think of Eddie and the other guys back home until I drowsed off.

Once, when Mother came upstairs to bring me a cold drink and to change my warm, rumpled pillow-case, I asked her how come Dad had bought such an inconvenient house. "Don't they have any modern ones in this town? Something more like our place back home?" She looked so tired.

"Darling, this place has charm," she said. "I think you'll like it once you're up and around."

"Whenever that is," I muttered.

"The doctor said it should just be a few more days."

"Until what?"

"You can get out of bed."

She left and I dozed off. When I opened my eyes, I saw my five-year-old sister, Colleen, standing in the doorway with a boy who looked about her age. She was holding a glass of lemonade.

"Who's your friend, Collie?" I asked.

"It's Eric," she said. "Come on in, Eric. He won't swear at you. Probably."

"What?" I asked.

"Well, you did, a few times when you were delicious."

"When I was—? Oh. You mean *delirious*. Out of my head. But you don't mean I swore at Eric? I don't even know him."

"But he heard you one time. Come on in, Eric." She handed me the glass of lemonade. It was sticky. "I made this myself," Colleen said. A layer of sugar had settled on the bottom.

Eric edged into the room. He was round faced, with large blue eyes and a rather small mouth. His flat hair was brownish blond, with bangs. "Hi," he said shyly.

"You live around here?" I asked. Not that I particularly cared, but it was a dull afternoon.

"He lives just across the street, don't you Eric?" my sister, Miss Kindergarten Social Chairman, said. "In that big house they're painting. Lots of colors, too."

"And how did you two happen to meet? Was it on some madcap adventure you'd like to tell the TV audience about?"

Eric looked baffled.

"He's just trying to be funny," my sister explained. "He was like this even before he got damaged in the brain from the fever."

"Oh. You want to see my house?" the boy asked.

"Sure, sometime."

Colleen said, "You could see it out of my window at the front, or out of Teresa's. Want to?"

"Some other time." I shifted around on the bed.

Colleen made a little face. "Come on, Eric. Let's go watch them paint." She paused at the door. "Now, I want to see you drink every drop of that lemonade."

As soon as they took off, I put down the glass. I could hear them clattering down the stairs and then I heard the front screen door slam. At home we'd had storm doors that never slammed shut.

I got up and turned the switch on the doorknob to lock the two of them out if they came back.

What kind of house was this, anyway? No wall-to-wall carpeting, no air conditioning. Even the electrical lines had to be revved up for our appliances. I wished I could close my eyes and open them back in our old house. I wished I could look up and see Eddie, and the rest of the guys. I wished we could all go out back and shoot baskets. Right now, the best I could do was shoot wadded-up tissues at the wastepaper basket. And miss most of the time.

This house was not my home. It was not where I wanted to be. You could take its charm and shove it. The stairs creaked and strange, whistling sounds came in the dead of night. There was something a bit weird about the place. I didn't think it would ever seem like home.

With those thoughts I must have dozed off. The next thing I knew, Mother was knocking at my door. I got up and let her in.

"Darling, you were moaning," she said. "Are you all right?"

"Oh, yeah. I had this . . . oh well, it doesn't matter."

I'd been dreaming it was night and I was in bed in an abandoned house, with the wind howling in through broken shutters. Greenish spirit shapes wafted into the room and gathered around me and were trying to draw me to them. I held tightly to the headboard but my grip was slipping and I was being pulled away . . . to where?

It was a dream, only a dream. But I couldn't shake it off.

Mother straightened my sheets, and then with a worried look finally left me alone.

I kicked the sheets loose and propped up the pillows against the headboard.

Using the remote, I turned on the TV across the room but there was just a lot of late-afternoon junk on one channel after another. The spirits I'd dreamed of hovered at the edge of my mind. I wished they'd go away. If I'd been well, they'd have been booted out the minute I opened my eyes.

Finally I found a baseball game in its ninth inning.

No Cubs, no White Sox, no Cardinals. It looked like some regional team, and who cared?

I was really deep into self-pity. There was nothing to look forward to here, no big event looming on the horizon. Dull, dull, dull, that's what my life was and probably would be forever.

There was no way for me to know that afternoon that really strange things were about to occur. Not right away, but soon.

T W O

*E*ach day I got to feeling a little stronger. I could stagger down the hall to the bath-room on my own now, without waiting for Mom or Dad to support me. I began sitting in a chair near the bed for a few hours each day. But I still wasn't allowed to go downstairs.

The high point of my day was when I called Eddie. The folks let me call him, but he wasn't allowed to call me long distance because of the expense. It was great at first, hearing his voice, finding out what was going on in the old neighborhood.

After a while, though, he didn't seem to be around as often when I called. He'd gone to town or he was over at Dave's house. Dave was a new guy who had a pool in his backyard. I realized before long that Eddie and I were running out of things to tell each other.

"That's the way it goes," Teresa said one day as she sat on the chair in my room, combing her long, dark hair still wet from a shampoo. "People drift apart."

"Not friends from kindergarten days."

Teresa shrugged. "I don't hear from Kristi, either."

"Kristi's a flake."

In the old days my sister would have pointed out that Eddie was some kind of lowlife, but ever since I'd been sick she'd tried to keep me from getting riled. I guess she didn't want to feel responsible if my temperature shot up.

"Anyway," I said, "you'll be seeing some of your friends when you go up North to college."

"True," she said, "but I hope to make new friends, too."

I knew she was implying that I should make new friends as well, but even if I'd been up and healthy I still wouldn't have wanted to.

Switching subjects, she said, "Have you seen the Painted Lady?"

"The *who?*"

"That house across the street that they're painting a lot of colors. It's really bizarre. You can see it from the front bedroom windows."

"Colleen mentioned it. I can wait."

Teresa seemed about to comment on my glumness, but she didn't. This was a new kind of attitude from a sister who used to tell me off regularly. Maybe she'd grow up to be more like Mother after all. She had the same Madonna look at times . . .

and I don't mean the entertainer, but the real saint that you see in paintings.

I used to wonder how Mom, who was so serene, and Dad, who was so gentle, had ever produced kids like us. It's strange. I'm tall, slim, and blond like Dad, and the girls all have Mom's dark good looks, but there the resemblance ends. Colleen, for example, is a little spitfire and I don't think she'll ever change.

Teresa, still combing her hair, got up and strolled to my farther window. "There's a nice, big meadow out there," she said. "It's completely empty. If this were back home, they'd be tearing it up and putting in another mall."

"You'd love that."

"Actually, it's rather sweet and dreamy just as it is. Makes me think of maidens in big hats wandering about, gathering armloads of flowers."

"Teresa, you were out in the sun too long today," I said, switching on the TV.

My sister took the hint and left. After she did, I eased out of bed and walked over to the window. I don't know where Teresa got that gathering-of-flowers bit. All I could see was a big expanse of weedy grass with trees along the far edge. What was beyond it, I had no idea. And I couldn't have cared less.

I made myself stay up so I'd be good and tired by bedtime. My nights, if I didn't nap too much during the day, were getting better. The fever seemed to stay away, and the dreams had settled down into standard stuff with nothing strange to sweat about.

♦

As usual, that evening Mother changed my damp, wrinkled sheets for cool, ironed ones. She'd had help every day since we moved, a Mrs. Tennyson who did a lot of the heavy work, including laundry.

Dad brought bowls of strawberry ice cream for the three of us, and by the time we ate that and talked for a while I was ready to stretch out and shut off the controls.

Dad switched off the fan because a sudden cool breeze was coming in the windows. He and Mom left, and in the darkened room I drifted off into a soothing, peaceful sleep.

Soon I was dreaming of a meadow filled with flowers. I was wandering around, wondering why I was there and whether I was supposed to pick the flowers or just look at them. As the dream continued I suddenly heard something. A scraping kind of sound. Where was it coming from? I looked around but couldn't see anything there in the meadow.

My mind pulled itself out of the dream, and I was back in my room, half-awake now. I could still hear whatever it was. I wanted to drift off to sleep again, but I couldn't because of the scraping noise, faint but persistent. Finally I shook myself all the way awake.

The sound was coming from the screened window

near my bed. The window was in shadow from the large oak tree outside, some of whose branches bordered the roof on the porch below.

It's only the wind, blowing a twig against the screen, I told myself. But the tree branch hadn't seemed that close to the window. Then my heart leaped a little as I thought, *It's Eddie. He's run away from home to come see me.*

"Eddie?" I said in a low voice.

There was no response, only more scratching sounds.

"Who's there?" Somehow I felt no fear.

I slid out of bed and crawled toward the window. Then I remembered the flashlight on my night table. I twisted around and got it and when I reached the window I turned it on.

The first thing I saw was what looked like two fireballs. Then I could see a whiteness surrounding them. I blinked in disbelief as I realized what was staring at me. A cat!

Most stray cats would run if a flashlight were turned on in their face but this one reached out and scraped the screen again. *Let me in* seemed to be its message.

I grasped the springs at each end of the screen and pushed up. When the screen had risen about eight inches I lost my balance and fell backward. At the same time the flashlight dropped and rolled out of reach.

As I lay there I heard a slight sound of padded

paws hitting the wooden floor. I could sense rather than see the cat's presence until my eyes adjusted, and then I could dimly make out the whitish glow of its fur. Strangest of all, the cat seemed to give off a scent of flowers.

I wished I could see it better. I felt around for the flashlight as the cat moved about the room. But then, behind me, I heard the tiniest sound as it leaped up to the sill. Before I could react, the cat was gone.

I crawled back to the window and peered out where the screen was lifted. Hard as I tried I couldn't see a thing except dark leaves and even darker branches. I started to lower the screen but stopped. Maybe it . . . the ghost cat . . . would return. I felt around for my bedside table lamp, turned it on, and retrieved the flashlight. I put it within reach on the table.

Lying in my bed again, I tried to guess where the cat might have come from and why it had jumped into my room. It seemed to ignore me, and want nothing in particular.

After this sudden, brief visitation, I had a hard time calming down. I began to feel a bit feverish and achy again. Kicking off the sheets, I flopped around on the bed trying to fall asleep, but I was still too intrigued by the strange visitor to let myself relax.

Finally I did drift off, and then the old nightmarish dreams came back. Once more I was struggling and fighting, trying to get somewhere but unable to free my legs from some sticky mire. I must have yelled, because suddenly I was awake and my parents were standing by me. When I looked down, I realized I was hanging on to the windowsill.

"What? What?" I mumbled, confused.

"Shhh, honey, you were dreaming," Mom said, taking hold of my arms.

"Here, son, come back to bed," Dad said. He turned on my light. To Mom he said, "He's soaked with sweat."

Dad gave me a dry T-shirt to put on while Mom smoothed out the sheets.

"What were you dreaming about?" Dad asked.

"Just crazy stuff."

"Well, you'll be all right now," he said. "Just put it out of your mind . . . relax."

I must have done just that because the next thing I knew, it was morning.

It puzzled me for a moment when I noticed the different shirt I was wearing—actually, it was on backward—and then I vaguely remembered yelling during the night and my parents coming into the room.

"I was trying to escape from something in my dream," I told Mom when she brought in my breakfast tray. "I remember clawing at some roots or trees, trying to catch hold of something solid."

"That explains why you were over at the window, hanging on for dear life."

I groaned. "Mom, am I losing my grip? On reality, I mean. Am I losing my mind?"

"Jon, darling. Of course not. It's just the fever."
She sat on the edge of the bed. "Back home you had
feverish dreams night and day for a while. But
you're so much better now."

"Am I going to get well?"

A startled look came over my mother's face. "Jon!
Of course you're going to get well."

"It's been so long now . . . all these weeks. I'm
really sick of it. Of being sick, I mean."

"I know. We lose patience with our bodies. Why
can't they do what they're supposed to do and let us
get on with our lives?"

"That's right."

She got up. "But believe me, you are getting a
little better every day, my pet. One of these days,
soon . . ."

"Sure." I tried to make it sound upbeat, but I was
beginning to wonder. Was I really getting better or
were some days just not as bad as others?

At least my appetite was improving. Cereal and
toast and eggs tasted as good as they had back home.
So far no one had tried to slip any southern stuff
onto my tray, although Eddie kept asking if I had
developed an appetite for hominy grits and biscuits
with gravy.

I poured milk onto my Wheaties and the whiteness suddenly triggered a faint memory. Cat. White
cat. *There had been a white cat in my room last night!*

Get a grip, I told myself.

I looked over at the window. Screen down as

usual. I looked at my bedside table. Flashlight standing upright the way it always did.

You were hallucinating, I told myself. *You are losing it.* There had been no cat in this room, white or otherwise. Why would a cat come into a strange place, where a strange person was sleeping? How would it have gotten on the roof? All right, it could have climbed up the tree. But why? Why, in the middle of the night, would a cat suddenly decide to pay a visit, scratch at a screen, and stroll around in a darkened room? It made no sense.

So, the cat's visit had been a small dream, a warm-up for the feature attraction: Jon trying to escape from unknown forces, yelling and waking up half the household.

I ate the cereal, the toast, and the eggs. Did I want the orange slices? Maybe . . . as soon as I shifted a bit and got more comfortable. When I moved, one of my knees hit the end of the tray. It tilted and the orange slices fell to the floor.

Saying a few words under my breath, I slid out of bed and picked up the fruit. And that's when I saw it. A flower. A tiny pink flower. Where had it come from? I'd never let Mom or Teresa put any flowers in my room.

A strange little shiver went up the back of my neck as I held the blossom and sniffed. It was real. And the cat was real too. I knew it because this was the very same flower scent I'd smelled last night, when the cat had walked into my room!

THREE

♦ ♦ ♦

"You look," Teresa said as she came in to pick up the tray, "like the cat that ate the canary."

"*What?*" I opened my bedside table drawer and, blocking my sister's view, tossed in the flower. Then I stood with my back to the table. "What do you mean by that?"

Teresa stared at me. "It's only an expression. Why are you acting so paranoid?"

"I'm not." I guess I was, though. "You just startled me, coming into the room like that."

She looked at me a moment longer, picked up the tray, and said, "Next time I'll belt out a few bars of 'Jailhouse Rock' as I come up the stairs."

"Excellent." I waited until Teresa had gone and then opened the drawer and looked at the flower again. Wow, it was weird the way that cat had come in, carrying a perfumy scent, as though it had passed through one of those department stores where sales clerks spritz the customers. But it had been an actual flower. I didn't get it. *How had the cat carried it? And why had it left it?*

I thought about this all the time I was down the hall taking a shower. No matter which way I tried to approach the incident, it just didn't make any sense. All I could do was wait and see if the cat came back again. And be ready if it did.

For lack of anything better to do, once I was dressed (that is to say, in clean sleepwear and robe) I sauntered into Colleen's room and looked over at the house across the street.

Painted Lady! That was an understated name if I ever heard one. What lunatic had been let loose with buckets of paint in every imaginable color? The main part of the house glowed with lavender. The shutters were flag blue. The porch pillars were the same brilliant blue with accents of green and orange. I've seen kindergarten paintings that displayed more color sense.

"Jon!" My little sister's voice came from behind me. "What are you doing in my room?"

"Well, Colleen, I'll tell you. I am looking at your friend Eric's house. You did invite me to look, remember?"

"Oh." She came to stand beside me. "Isn't it scrumptious?"

"That's a word," I agreed. Not the one I'd have chosen. "How come they're doing that? Using all those colors?"

Colleen shrugged. "Because they wanted to. Eric's so lucky. I wish we lived in a house like that."

"But when he's inside he can't see it. While you, over here, can look at it all day long. So you're the one who hits the jackpot." *Why was I saying this?*

My sister screwed up her face with heavy thought. "You're right," she said then. She paused and suddenly her face lighted up. "I know! We can get Mommy and Dad to have our house painted, too! Then Eric can look at ours, and we can look at his!"

Oh, wonderful, I thought. *The folks will have a little something else to contend with.* "I wouldn't bring it up just now, Colleen," I said. "They've got a lot on their minds. Why don't you hold your suggestion for a while?" *Like forever.*

"Okay." Colleen yanked off the ribbon that had slid halfway off her ponytail and handed it to me to retie. "What are you going to do today?"

"My plans?" Since when did I have any plans? "Well first, Colleen, I thought I'd finish up my blueprints for a space platform designed to carry a city full of people, with plazas, high rises, parks, you know. And after that . . ."

"Want to play crazy eights?"

"Sure, why not?"

Delighted at my easy consent, Colleen dashed to her bookcase for the cards and we sat cross-legged on her bed for some heated rounds. She won, as always. Also, as always, she was not what you'd call a modest winner. When I really concentrated, hoping to squelch her a little, she still triumphed . . . with squeals of delight.

"I give up," I said finally. "I'm tired."

"Tired of losing?" Her smile was downright wicked.

"I guess. Learn to play blackjack, kid, and you can clean up in Vegas." I went back to my room, turned on the fan, and stretched out on my bed. Then I leaned over and opened the drawer to look at the flower once again. Still there, still very real. And still very mystifying.

That afternoon I called Eddie's house again, and he was actually there for a change.

"So Jon, what's new?" he asked.

I'd had every intention of telling him about the strange cat that had come through the window, walked around my room, and left, leaving behind a flower. But suddenly I felt myself unwilling to share the experience. I wanted to keep this secret to myself, at least for a while.

"There's not a lot going on," I said. Briefly, I thought of mentioning the house across the street, but Eddie would probably think that a pathetic subject.

"How do you like living in the South by now?" he asked.

"Fine," I said. And before he could mention it, "Still eating northern food. We have it brought in by dogsled."

Eddie laughed. "How does you sister like it?"

I was surprised he was interested. "You know Colleen. She thinks the universe revolves around her no matter where she lives."

"No, I meant Teresa."

I'd forgotten that Eddie had a lifelong crush on my older sister. A hopeless crush. She's three years older and considers him an insignificant blob.

"She misses you a lot," I said.

"Like a zit."

"No, more like a disgusting growth, with hairs sprouting out and little—"

"Okay, okay. So, tell her I said hello. No, don't. So, are you up and around?"

"A little. What's new there?"

"Not much. Same old thing."

There was a silence when I guess both of us realized we had nothing more to say. Finally, with a lame "Well, I gotta get going," Eddie brought the nonconversation to a close.

After we'd hung up I leaned back on my pillows with a feeling of sadness coming over me. Was this all that was left of Eddie's and my friendship? We two who had been inseparable all these years?

We knew stuff about each other that no one else knew. We'd covered for each other in times of stress. We'd gone through secret clubs and secret codes, shared an attraction for ancient Egypt and, on a contemporary plane, a girl new to the school. We'd taken turns winning at tennis and chess.

When I first got sick with rheumatic fever, Eddie used to stop by every day after school to keep me up to date on what was happening. I don't mean studies. A tutor came around for that. Eddie kept me informed about the subculture of school. He was the kind of guy who blended into and was welcomed by any group and always seemed to be well thought of, though not for any one particular reason. He was just himself. Eddie. No pretensions. He was what he seemed to be.

Well, he seemed to be slipping out of my life and there was nothing I could do about it. Not now. Not while my life consisted of degrees of temperature and joint aches. Up or down. Maybe when I was back to normal we could pick up on our interests and get some real conversations going again.

When I felt better I'd go to the library and check out some new science fiction. That'd be something to discuss over the phone. Maybe Eddie could come on a visit during a school holiday. Seeing each other should get our stalled friendship into gear again and move it forward.

But first, I had to build up my strength and endurance. Then maybe I could get back to being an interesting person.

♦

For the first time since we had moved into the house, I was going to be allowed to go downstairs for dinner.

"Come along, son," Dad said after I'd put on a robe over my pajamas. "I'll help."

"I can walk alone," I said. "I'm not an invalid."

"You're doing fine," he said, standing aside, ignoring my irritable tone.

Why, I wondered, as we went down the stairs, did I have to snap at him that way? All through my entire sickness he'd been calm and agreeable. There were times, sure, when the pain made me a little crazy, but at other times I'd acted like a jerk just because I felt like it. One of these days I ought to make it up to Dad, or at least show some appreciation.

Eating at the dining room table instead of off a tray was such a trip—*Wow, I can eat with my feet on the floor and my elbows on the table!*—that I didn't pay any attention to Collie's inane prattle until I heard Teresa ask her, "What crazy girl?"

"The one who used to live around here," Colleen said.

As we all stared at my sister, I asked, "What are you talking about?"

Colleen flung out her arms, palms up, in the gesture made famous by Michael Jordan, and said in her own dramatic way, "I am telling all you folks what Eric told me. A girl lived in this town who was off in her upper story."

"Colleen, that's not a nice thing to say," my mother told her.

"Especially about someone you don't know," my father added.

"Besides," Teresa joined in, "I'd consider the source. Your Eric impresses me as being a little out to lunch himself."

Colleen reared up from her chair. "Don't you talk about my friend like that!"

"Oh, please," Teresa said. "You've known him for how long?"

"That's enough," Dad said. "Sit down, Colleen."

Mother sighed. "Let's try to have a pleasant meal. It's Jon's first time in this dining room."

Colleen gave me a look from under her frowning eyebrows and muttered a little, but no one paid any attention. In a few minutes she was prattling away again, this time about the new color that had appeared on the Painted Lady that day. I don't know if my little sister's mood changes mean she has a sweet, forgiving nature or Jell-O for brains. Anyway, that was all that was said about the so-called crazy girl at dinner and I think most of us forgot about it.

Later, though, in bed, I had a feeling . . . a squirmy feeling under my scalp . . . that something was not right about this neighborhood. Or, more specifically, this house. I had absolutely nothing to base the feeling on, but still it was there. Did this place have a history? Had something gone on before we came— maybe years ago, actually—that we had never heard about? I wondered how long the house had been vacant before my naive northern parents bought it.

Maybe I could ask Mrs. Tennyson the next time she came to clean. I'd got off on the wrong foot with her my first day here. She'd walked into my room with some roses from her garden and I'd yelled at her to take them away. I told her I didn't need flowers, I wasn't dying. A hurt expression came over her face and she left.

The next time I saw her, I apologized, saying the roses had reminded me of the ones I'd seen at my grandmother's funeral last year.

"Well, now, don't you worry about that," Mrs. Tennyson had said. Then she'd gone on to tell me how her various relatives had survived any number of peculiar ailments.

Now, I decided, pulling up the sheet, I'd ask the woman some specific questions about this house the first chance I had.

I felt very tired from being downstairs. Would I fall into a deep sleep, too deep to hear the cat if it came back and scratched on the screen?

Rather than take that chance, I slid out of bed, went to the window, and raised the screen several inches. The cat would have free passage into my room. I'd just trust that I would wake up.

Back in bed that creepy feeling crept under my scalp again. There *was* something going on. I felt it. There was something truly eerie about this house.

I know I was still awake at ten o'clock, because I could hear very faintly the TV news coming on downstairs. Then I must have drifted off.

I don't know what time it was when I felt something moving about on my bed.

I lay perfectly still. I could feel the paw pressure coming closer to my face. Now it was by my shoulder. I looked sideways, still not moving. It began to purr.

"Kitty?" I said softly. It put a paw on my shoulder.

"Hi there," I said, still softly. "Where did you come from, kitty?"

My eyes were adjusting to the darkness. I could make out its form and the white fur. And there was something else . . . the scent of flowers.

Now I shifted ever so slightly. And slowly, so as not to startle it, I moved my hand toward the cat. It stayed still.

I touched its head. It made a little forward motion that seemed to indicate it was okay to pet it. I did. And then I moved my hand under its chin. Flowers. There was a wreath of flowers around its neck!

After a few moments I inched my body sideways toward the night table, and slowly, slowly, reached out for the flashlight.

I carefully turned it on, keeping the light shining away from the cat. Then I moved the beam until it crossed over my bed and finally shone close to but not directly on the cat. The animal was in profile now. Its eye was blue.

The cat turned its head to look at me and I stared at it, startled. The other eye was amber colored.

"Wow," I said. And at that, the cat leaped from my bed, sprang to the windowsill, and disappeared. It must have gone down the tree.

I got out of bed, flashlight in hand. If there had been a full moon I might have been able to see the cat, but the night was dark. The light from my flashlight ended at the edge of the roof with nothing but the tree's dark foliage beyond.

I went back to bed, trembling.

Whose cat was it, anyway? It had to belong to someone. Cats don't weave wreaths and put them around their own necks. But why did it come into my room? What was it looking for?

I turned on the bedside lamp and looked around on my sheets. There were a couple of petals that had fallen from the wreath. I put them into the table drawer with the flower from the night before. After that I lay there waiting, but the cat didn't return.

◆

The next day I thought about the strange white cat a lot. Who could I ask about it, without revealing that it had come into my room? Eric was a pretty sorry person to question, but he was the only outside contact I had in the neighborhood.

Naturally, just because I wanted to see him, he didn't show up. I decided to go into Colleen's room and see if he was out watching them paint his house.

I looked out the window but there was no sign of the kid.

A painter was doing the front steps now. Unbelievable! Along with a lavender, blue, green, and orange, a banana yellow was now being added.

"Oh . . ." Colleen called out from the hall. "In my room again!" She came over beside me, followed by the faithful Eric.

"Yeah, I just can't seem to keep away. That house is stupendously nausea making. And I mean that in the finest sense of the word," I told them.

Colleen and Eric regarded me, uncertain about what I'd actually said. Apparently my sincere look was reassuring. "You could see it better with binoculars," Colleen said.

Not a bad idea. Binoculars. I immediately thought of another, better use for them. "Where are they?" I asked.

"I'll go ask Mom."

Colleen streaked from the room and after a moment of indecision, Eric followed.

By the time they came back I had figured out how to extract information from the boy without telling him anything.

I took the binoculars from my sister and focused them. For a while I made half-assed comments about the house, how impressed I was, and so forth. Then I said, "Whose dog is that?"

"What dog?" Colleen wanted to know.

"Oh, he's gone now." I handed the glasses to my sister and casually asked Eric, "Are there lots of dogs in the neighborhood? I never hear any barking."

"There's one over on Magnolia Street. It's a boxer. They call it Champ."

"Fine name," I said.

"And Lee Tracy has a dog. I don't know what kind it is and I forget its name."

"How about cats?"

"Yeah, there're some."

I was trying to think of a way to pin Eric down without appearing too interested when he blurted out, "The crazy girl used to have a cat. It was spooky. It was an odd-eyed cat."

Colleen lowered the binoculars and laughed. "There's no such thing as an odd-eyed cat, Eric. You're so silly."

The boy flushed under this unexpected attack from his idol. "There is, too," he said. "That ole white cat had one blue eye and one brown eye."

A slight chill went through me. Could it be the same cat that had paid me those visits? It had to be. Odd-eyed cats aren't all that common.

Colleen favored the boy with her best stare. "Are you pulling my leg, Eric Andrew Stoneworth?"

"No, I am not."

"Let up, Colleen," I said. "I've heard of odd-eyed cats. They're always white and they're a regular breed. I remember a friend telling me about one he saw at a cat show a long time ago." Those words surfaced on their own. I'd forgotten all that stuff until now.

Colleen flicked a look at me but said sternly to Eric, "Show me the cat. Then I'll believe it."

"I can't. It belonged to the crazy girl and she's gone."

"Gone where?" Colleen asked.

"I don't know." Eric improvised. "Maybe she's dead."

"Dead, like in the cemetary?" Colleen asked.

"That's the only kind of dead there is," the boy said, blinking.

I don't know why, but his words made me break out in a cold sweat.

"Well." Colleen handed the binoculars to me. Whenever she's about to go down in defeat she does the sensible thing—changes the subject. "Jon, you never use it, so could I borrow it?"

"Borrow what?" I asked, my mind somewhere else.

Colleen sighed, as if her patience were being sorely tried. "Your camera, of course."

"I'm not sure it has any film," I said absently. Was the girl dead? And had the cat belonged to her? Then why . . .?

"I'll get film!"

I was conscious of Colleen flying out of the room and the sound of my dresser drawer slamming shut. "Come on, Eric, I've got it!" She yelled from the hall. I turned to see her waving the camera over her head, strap flapping. Eric ran to her.

Normally, I'd have shouted for her to be careful with it, but my mind was racing ahead, thinking of how later on I'd get the camera back and keep it on my bedside table next to the flashlight.

It wasn't clear to me what shots I hoped to take. I just had the feeling that strange events were about to take place, and I wanted to be ready.

FIVE

◆ ◆ ◆

*W*ith the binoculars, the flashlight, and the camera I'd got back from Colleen placed on my bedside table, I waited for the night. Things didn't look good as far as another visit from the cat was concerned. At about seven o'clock it started to rain, and as time went on, instead of letting up it only rained harder. There was even some thunder and occasional flashes of lightning.

Even to me, a guy who knew little about cats, it was clear the white cat wouldn't come calling that night. I slept restlessly, dozing and waking and dozing again. Maybe it was the storm. Maybe it was something weird about the house. Or maybe it was something weird about me.

Which led me to think again of the so-called crazy girl. Did she exist, or had Eric just made her up? If she was real, had she gone away? Or had she, as Eric suggested, died? But if she was a goner, who had made that wreath for her cat? If it *was* her cat.

◆

When I woke up, the sun was throwing a large rectangle of light through the far window. I went over and raised it, and the air outside felt sodden and heavy from last night's rain. There were still damp spots on the roof.

Mom brought in my breakfast tray and set it on a small table next to a chair.

"Mom," I said, "why don't you give yourself a break? I can go downstairs for breakfast now. I'm almost back to normal."

"Jon, don't rush it. It's better to build up your strength gradually . . ." She smoothed the bed sheets. "Did you take your temperature?"

"Yep. It's not even a degree over nincty-eight point six."

"Good. Dr. Arlo's coming by sometime this morning. Maybe he'll adjust your medication."

◆

The doctor didn't make that change, but he did seem pleased when he took my temperature and pulse and listened to my heart.

"How are the joints? Still having pain?" he asked, bending my knee.

"Very little," I told him. The doctor reminded me

of a hand puppet Colleen used to have. He had thick, dark eyebrows and a thick, dark mustache that ended abruptly, with no twirled ends. "When can I break out of here?" I asked.

"Anytime you feel like it."

"I can?" Wildly, I thought of hopping on a plane and flying up to see Eddie.

"For a few hours," he added, as though guessing what was racing through my mind. "No wild parties. No jitterbugging."

Jitterbugging? What kind of time warp was he in?

"I'll see that Jon doesn't overdo," Mom said. "Thank you, Doctor, for coming around. I know house calls are almost a thing of the past."

"Not here they aren't," the doctor said with a smile and just a trace of southern accent.

When he finally left, I didn't leap up as I'd imagined I might. Instead, I took a little nap to make up for sleep lost during last night's storm.

I did go downstairs for lunch, though, and later, in robe and slippers, sat on the creaking porch swing that the previous owners had left behind.

Colleen and Eric came and sat on the porch steps. My sister, wearing red shorts and an abbreviated printed top, gave me a critical look. "Aren't you embarrassed about what you're wearing?" she asked. "Out here where people can see you?"

"People can see most of *you*," I replied. "Isn't that kind of embarrassing?"

Collie glanced down at her bare legs and her bare midriff. She hugged herself around the waist and said, "Let's go to the cemetery, Eric."

"Why?" he asked.

"Yes, why?" I echoed. "I should think things would be dead enough for you right here."

She ignored that remark and stood up. "Well, do you want to or not?"

"Right now?" Eric huddled on the steps.

Colleen put her hands on her hips and glared. "You're not *afraid* are you, Eric Andrew Stoneworth?"

I shuddered to think of the contempt my sister would put into her voice when she really hit her stride . . . as a teenager.

Poor Eric looked dazed. Manfully, though, he stood up and said, "I'm not afraid. I just don't know why we have to go to the cemetery."

Colleen sighed. "To see if that crazy girl is buried there. Her grave marker might say, *Here lies the* . . . well, I guess they'd use her name instead of *crazy girl* . . . anyway, *What's-her-name. And cat.*"

"What makes you think her cat died, too?" I asked my sister.

"Of heartbreak. I'm sure it did."

"Oh, Colleen, you are so muddy in your thinking."

Without favoring me with a reply, my sister started down the front walk. "I'm going, Eric," she called back. "You don't have to."

After pausing a moment, Eric dragged after Colleen. Obviously, his fear of the cemetery paled in comparison to the fear of losing face with his friend.

"Hey, come back here!" I called out when I saw they were really going.

They both stopped and turned.

"Where is this cemetery, Eric?"

He pointed toward the meadow that started just beyond our house. "Down that way and over." He pointed to his left.

"You'd better ask Mom before you go, Colleen. I mean it!"

She stood glaring at me for a few moments, then stomped into the house. She came flying out just a minute or so later, gave Eric's shoulder a slap as she flew by him, and ran toward the meadow. Her friend chugged after her.

Later on, I found out that my sister had simply asked if she could walk in the meadow.

I continued to sit on the swing, one leg crossed over my knee, the other foot touching the porch just enough to make the swing move. I rather liked the squeak of the rusty chains and springs.

My back was toward the meadow so I didn't see the woman who came from it until she was on a level with me, out where the sidewalk begins. Or ends, depending on which way you're walking.

As I was wondering how the woman happened to be there, she turned and came up the walk toward the porch. Even though it was a hot day, she was wearing a print dress with long sleeves and a high neck. It was an old lady's kind of dress, but the woman looked to be in her thirties.

I had stopped the swing with my foot by the time she reached the porch. If she noticed me, she didn't show it. Her face was covered with freckles. Maybe that's why she kept her arms shielded from the sun. She rang the doorbell and Mom came to the door right away, as though she'd been expecting the woman.

"Mrs. Winger?" Mom asked, opening the screen door.

"Yes. I've come about the drapes."

"I'm so happy to meet you," Mom said. "I'm Katherine Connor. Come right in." Mom noticed me and would have introduced me, I know, but the woman was already in the house.

Colleen's comment about what I was wearing came back to me. *Maybe I should get dressed and drop the invalid bit,* I thought. When I walked into the house, I saw Mother and the sewing woman in the living room measuring the windows. I decided a soda would be a good idea and went to the kitchen to get one. I was heading for the stairs when Colleen and Eric bounded into the hall, slamming the screen door as always.

"Back so soon?" I asked. "Have a nice outing?"

"We couldn't stay there," Colleen said, "because some men were digging."

"A grave!" Eric said, eyes rounded.

"Sounds logical, in a cemetery," I said, taking a swig from the can. "Scared you, huh?"

"No, it didn't!" Colleen said. "We just . . . who's that in there with Mom?"

Before I could answer, Eric stepped backward, covered his mouth with his hand, and made a little sound. "It's . . . it's . . ."

"Well, who?" Colleen demanded.

Eric ducked behind the stairs and peered carefully through the railings. He pulled back into the shadows as Mrs. Winger and Mother came into the hall and then went out on the front porch, where they stood talking.

"That's who?" Colleen whispered to the still-shrinking Eric.

"The crazy girl's mother. That's who."

Again, a shiver went through me. Maybe it was because the kids had set out to look for the girl in the cemetery, and now, here was her mother. It was almost . . . I don't know. Too much of a coincidence. Why had the woman come to our house this particular afternoon?

Get a grip, I told myself. She had come, obviously, because Mom had called and asked her to come. She was a seamstress, after all, and Mother needed curtains for the living room windows.

I walked past Colleen and Eric, still whispering at the foot of the stairs, and went up to my room. As though pulled by some force, I crossed to the bedside table and opened the drawer. The flower petals were still there.

I held them in my palm and studied them. The flowers, the cat, the girl, the mother. And yes, this house. There was something strange about them all. Not supernatural. I didn't believe in any of that garbage. But still, something strange.

The odd-eyed cat held the clue, I was sure of that. He'd come to my room two times. Surely he'd return . . . maybe tonight, now that it had stopped raining.

In the meantime I'd go ahead and change clothes and then head downstairs to see if I could dig up some information about Mrs. Winger, the cat, or the girl.

*D*ownstairs I found Mom in the kitchen along with Mrs. Tennyson, who was ironing sheets. Good, I thought. Two to quiz at once.

"Who was that woman who was here just now?" I asked, tossing my empty soda can into the recycling bag.

"Mrs. Winger?" Mom looked up from her recipe notebook. "She's going to make new draperies for the living room. By the time they're ready I'll have had the room repainted."

"Not, I hope, by the guys who're doing the house across the street."

Mrs. Tennyson gave a little laugh. "I swear, those poor men will be crazy as coots by the time they're finished. Such nonsense, doing up a house that way."

Mom smiled. "Lorraine—Eric's mother—told me they've entered their house in a statewide contest for the most original use of color. She's pushing the men to get the work done before the judges come around."

"When's that?" I asked, opening the refrigerator to look for something interesting.

"I don't know." Mom began talking to Mrs. Tennyson about a recipe.

It would've seemed strange if I'd tried to turn the conversation back to Mrs. Winger, so I went into the living room, taking a bunch of grapes along.

After a while Mrs. Tennyson headed upstairs with a load of sheets and pillowcases. I gave her a minute and then wandered up to my room.

I was standing at my far window, looking out, when the cleaning woman brought in some of the linens to put into my drawer.

"What's over there?" I asked, pointing. "Beyond the meadow."

"Nothing much. Just an old house."

"Who owns it? Mrs. Winger, the woman who's making the curtains?"

"She's lived there for a few years, but she just rents. They say she's a real good seamstress. Keeps to herself and so does that sister she has living with her. Peculiar woman. Would you like your sheets changed now?"

"Sure. If you don't mind." I wanted to keep Mrs. Tennyson in the room, talking. "How is the sister peculiar?"

"Mutters to herself, walking down the street. Sits in the library reading all kinds of odd books about the occult, mysteries of the universe, things like that. Or so I've been told. Grows rare herbs and sells them to that new fiddly-faddly health store run by a bunch of flakes."

"Lots of people are into herbs now," I said.

"That may be, but the devil alone knows what evil weeds some of them are."

"You mean like pot?"

"Oh lordy no, the authorities would shut 'em down faster than an owl could hoot if they tried to sell pot!"

I picked up a kaleidoscope someone had given me when I was in the hospital and held it to my eye. Nonchalantly I said, "I hear Mrs. Winger had a daughter who died."

"What?" The housekeeper snapped a sheet over the bed. "Who told you that nonsense?"

I lowered the kaleidoscope. "Little Eric from across the street."

"Oh, well. The girl disappeared, that's all. If she'd died I'm sure we would've heard about it." Mrs. Tennyson finished making the bed and scooped up the dirty linens from the floor. "It sure is good to see you up and around, boy. You had your poor mama and papa worried near to death when you first got here."

"I'm sorry about that. But I'm fine now."

"All right, but you just take care. Don't overdo."

She started to leave the room but stopped when I asked, "Who lived in this house before us?" That might give me some more clues.

"Who?" Mrs. Tennyson shifted the bundle of linens. "Well, let me think. It's been empty for quite some years. The folks' name was Branson, I believe. Before that, I don't remember." She took a step back into the room and frowned slightly. "A pair of brothers built the place, way back when. Strange men, I've been told."

More strange people. Did this place attact them or what? "How were they strange?" I asked.

"Deathly afraid of fire. Wanted to build a fire escape from upstairs here, but the zoning laws wouldn't allow it. I guess they worked out something else, but I don't know what. Both died of natural causes."

"A long time ago," I said, partly to reassure myself.

"That's right—a very long time ago." She turned and left.

I thought over what Mrs. Tennyson had told me. The girl, the house, the cat. They all seemed connected but I didn't know how.

◆

We ate a little early that night because my parents were going out to their first social event since we'd moved here. Dad's boss's wife was having a little gathering.

"Don't stay up too late," Mother said to me as they were leaving. "You don't want to tire yourself and have the fever come back."

"I won't." God, I was so sick of all this. "Tell Colleen she can't stay up all night, either."

"We already have," Dad said. He called to my sister sitting cross-legged before the TV, "Don't forget. When that show's over, you go to bed, Colleen."

"Yeah." She didn't bother to turn her head.

The folks left and Teresa came down the stairs. "Let's sit on the porch for a while, Jon. Okay?"

I put my hands to my chest in mock surprise. "Me? You want *me* to keep you company?"

"Only because there's no one else."

We went out and sat on the swing. It was rather muggy outside but once in a while a little breeze stirred the air. I turned my wristwatch toward the light from inside. Only eight o'clock. Plenty of time before the cat would come around. If it did that night . . .

Teresa sighed, and got the swing moving. "It's such a drag, moving down here and not knowing anybody and you being sick and everything."

"Sorry." Meaning, *What kind of drag do you think it's been for me?*

"It's not your fault," she said charitably. "But Dad has been so busy with the new job and Mom's been tied up with you and the house. I feel so alone. And I miss Ace."

"You'll see a lot of him at college this fall."

"I want to go out on dates *now*."

"So find another boyfriend."

"Oh, sure. Thanks."

I felt a little sorry I'd said that. Teresa probably

didn't want a new love interest any more than I wanted a new best friend.

"I miss Eddie, too," I commented.

My sister didn't seem to hear. "I sometimes wonder if he's dating someone else. There were dozens of girls dying to go out with him."

"Call and ask him, why don't you?"

"Oh, sure, and have him lie."

"I think Eddie has made new friends since I left," I said.

"Eddie? It's not the same thing. Ace and I have been together for years."

I could've reminded Teresa that Eddie and I had been friends since kindergarten, but she didn't want to hear that. She just wanted to sound off to someone and I was handy.

"Maybe you could fly up to see Ace," I suggested.

Teresa stopped the swing so suddenly I almost pitched out. "See? That seems perfectly logical to you, doesn't it? Why can't Mom and Dad see it?"

"Hey, look, I didn't mean . . ."

"I could stay at Allison's and see Ace and find out how he feels about me, really. That way, when I go off to college this fall I'll know where I stand with him."

"Wouldn't it save time and money to ask him that on the phone?"

"Oh, forget it." Teresa put the swing back into motion.

We didn't talk for a while. I knew what she was thinking about, and I began wondering about Eddie again. Was I out of his life? I could see that things had to be different, with me living way down here in the South. But couldn't he pick up the phone and call me, even if his parents made him pay for it?

"I think I may have a job," Teresa said. "For the rest of the summer. At a fast-food place."

"You're lucky. To have the energy to work."

Teresa suddenly seemed to view me as something more than a listening post. "I thought you were feeling better."

"I am. But even if I were old enough to put in an eight-hour day I couldn't. I wear down fast."

"Poor baby." She briefly touched my arm and then leaned back and ran her fingers through her long hair. "I've been thinking how hard it's been for everyone to help take care of you. But I guess you've suffered, too."

I didn't have an answer to that . . . a civil answer . . . so I just kept quiet. After a while Teresa decided to go inside and give herself a facial.

It was a dreamy kind of night. Or maybe I'd slipped into a state of altered consciousness. I felt like I was in some new place for the first time, and yet it was familiar. The moon, of course, was familiar, but the scent in the air, though nice, was different from the smell of summer back home.

Alone, and fully dressed for a change, I decided to take a little stroll. I walked down our front walk to the sidewalk. There was an empty lot to the left of our house, but beyond were a few houses—only three on the rest of our block. From in front of the empty lot I got a good view of Eric's Painted Lady house across the street, but the colors were muted by the night.

I turned back and walked across the front of our house to where the sidewalk ended. Then I walked on a little way into the meadow. There was nothing much to see—just grass and trees.

I went back to the house and up to my room. Colleen, for a wonder, seemed to be asleep when I checked, and Teresa had her bedroom door closed.

Later, lying in bed in my darkened room, with the screen raised, I hoped for the cat's return. Finally I thought I heard a sound on the roof, but wouldn't you know . . . right then my telephone rang!

Wrong number. Great. I was so annoyed I couldn't fall asleep after that. I was still awake when my parents came home around midnight. At two o'clock I was still awake. If the cat came after that, I was too zonked out to know it.

◆

Two more nights passed. The third night I was waiting as usual, screen raised, lights out.

I heard a small scratching suddenly, on the windowsill. Then there was a tiny rushing sound, and a weight landed on the bed beside me. I lay perfectly still as the cat paused, possibly to test my reaction. I felt it walking around my legs, then up toward my shoulder. I could smell the faint scent of flowers once again. Finally the cat daintily stepped upon my chest and settled there.

I raised my head as much as I could, lying on my back, and stared straight into the face of the cat. Its eyes gleamed, but in the darkness of the new moon I could not make out their blue and amber colors.

"Whose cat are you?" I whispered. "Where do you come from? Who sent you here?" I was shivering slightly.

The cat began purring and settled itself more comfortably on my chest. I made no movement for fear of frightening it off. It seemed to be about ten minutes, but it could have been less, that the cat lay there and purred. Suddenly it sat up, turning its head toward the window. And then I heard it.

"Cat, cat," a soft voice was calling. It sounded very near, from the tree outside, or maybe the roof. "Cat . . . cat . . ."

Who was that? What was going on here? With pin-pricks traveling up and down my spine in a crazy rhythm, I gently moved the cat off my chest and got out of bed. I knelt down and crawled toward the open window. I reached the sill and slowly raised my head. And gasped.

There was a face looking at me from the roof!

I reared back and took a couple of deep breaths. Then I raised myself up again. Now I could see more clearly. It was a girl's face, her hair transformed by rays of moonlight into a hazy mist. I could barely make out her features.

"Wh . . . who are you?" I managed to gasp.

"I'm Flora, of course." Her voice was light and breathy.

Flora, of course. As if I were supposed to know her. "Wh . . . what do you want?"

"My cat. He's in there. I know he is."

"He's your cat?"

"Would you please stop asking questions and give him to me."

"He's free to go anytime he likes," I said, and realized I sounded like a policeman. I was shaken, though. I mean, first a strange odd-eyed cat appeared, and now this girl who seemed like a spirit of the night.

"He came in just to visit, I guess." Spirit or not, I didn't want this girl-creature to think I had set some kind of lure for her cat.

"He's always liked that room."

"My room?" How strange. "Did he . . . and you live here once?"

"No, of course not. It's where we hid out. But I haven't time to go into that now."

The cat came over then and leaped to the sill.

"Oh, Cat, Cat, you shouldn't run off like that," Flora said, gathering him up.

She released the cat and it raced toward the tree

and disappeared down the trunk. The girl started after it.

"Wait . . ." I called out in a hoarse whisper.

She turned.

"My name is Jon."

I could see her only as a shadowy form when she said airily, "All right, it's Jon. Anything else?"

"I . . . I wish you'd come back sometime, with Cat."

"I might. It would have to be late, though. At night." She vanished into the leaves of the tree. I listened, but couldn't hear her drop from the lower branch to the ground.

I hurried over to my other window to try to see where they were headed. I could make out the girl's figure going toward the meadow, but I couldn't see the cat. Then I rushed to my bedside table and scrabbled around for the binoculars. By the time I found them and held them to my eyes, there was no one outside to see.

I could feel my heart racing. Too stirred up to go back to bed, I pulled my chair close to the window and stared at the now empty meadow. Was this Flora the so-called crazy girl? She hadn't seemed crazy to me. Strange, though, the way she'd come right up to my window without being the least bit afraid. Of course, she knew the room if she'd hid out in here.

Why? Who had she been hiding from?

She could only come back at night, she'd said. So obviously she was still hiding. Again I wondered— from whom?

Was the cat in hiding, too?

For the first time in weeks I felt my blood pulsing . . . not from sickness now, but from excitement and anticipation.

What would happen next? I had no idea. And I couldn't wait to find out.

♦　♦　♦

I woke up feeling exhilarated. *My life has defi-nitely taken on a new rush,* I thought, as I jogged downstairs.

"Well, look who's up and fully dressed for a change," Teresa commented. "Does this mean we can retire the trays and room service?"

"For now," I said. "Unless people start hassling me and send me into a relapse." I pulled out a chair and sat at the table.

"Have you decided not to be sick anymore?" Colleen inquired.

"You gnat. I never *decided* to be sick. I just was."

Dad looked at me through his round silver-rimmed glasses, and smiled. "It's good to see you coming back," he said. "We were worried there for a while."

Mom touched me lightly on the shoulder as she poured my orange juice. "Worried, but always optimistic," she said.

"Sit down," I told her. "You don't have to wait on me all the time."

"Yes, Mother," Teresa said. "Jon's pathetic invalid role has grown a little old and ragged. You should start taking it easy yourself. You've been doing too much."

I felt like telling my sister it wouldn't kill her to hang around the house and give Mom a hand instead of going off to some job. But I didn't want to start anything.

Later, I helped Mom with the dishes, sitting on a stool and drying as she washed. "When will the curtains be done?" I asked, reaching around to put a teapot into the cupboard.

"Not right away. Why?" Mom asked.

"Just wondered."

"Actually, Mrs. Winger doesn't even have the fabric yet. It arrived yesterday afternoon. I'm going to drop it off later today."

"You are?" For a moment I visualized my mother driving through the meadow, but there had to be a more conventional way to get to Flora's house. "Maybe I'll ride along," I said.

"That would be wonderful. You haven't seen anything of this town."

"I know." I hung up the damp dish towel. "What time are you leaving?"

"After lunch. Mrs. Tennyson won't be here today, and I have to wait around for the dishwasher repairman this morning."

"Oh." I wandered outside to the backyard. It was big and with work could be quite nice. There were a couple of trees that would be perfect for a hammock slung between them.

The people before us must have had a vegetable garden toward the back, but it was all weeds now. It's ironic. When I was healthy, working in a garden was about the last thing I wanted to do in this world. But now all I could think was how great it'd be to have the energy to do it.

I strolled toward the front of the house, passing by the huge tree outside my bedroom window. It would take a bit of hoisting to get up to the first big fork, and then a lot of scrambling from one branch to another to reach the flat roof. That Flora, I thought, must be surefooted. Of course, to her cat the climb would be nothing.

I made a few attempts to climb up to the big fork but my arms started trembling. I could get the step stool from the kitchen, but what would be the point? Besides, I didn't want to draw anyone's attention to the tree.

I walked around to the front of the house and took a few steps into the meadow.

"Are you going to the cemetery?"

I wheeled around. Oh. It was only Colleen.

"Me? Cemetery? Why would you think that?" For a weird moment I connected it with my being sick.

Colleen gave me her exasperated look. "To see if the crazy girl's there, of course."

"Would you just get that out of your head, Colleen? There's no crazy girl, dead or otherwise. And how come you're all smeared with paint?"

"They let Eric and me paint a banister, on the back porch, where hardly anyone can see. Come on, Jon, come look at the house."

Avoiding the paint-smeared hand my sister was holding out, I walked across the street with her. Up close the house looked like a colorized nightmare.

A woman came out of the front door.

"Hello there," she said. "You must be Colleen's poor sick brother. It's good to see you up and about."

"Hi. I'm Jon. I'm not really sick anymore."

"This is Eric's mother," Colleen piped up.

Mrs. Stoneworth held out her hand. "Pleased to meet you at last. You can just call me Lorraine."

We shook hands. She looked awfully young to be someone's mother, although of course Eric wasn't all that old. Her light-colored hair was pulled back with a big bow, and she was wearing a flouncy kind of top and skinny pants with a floral design.

"I guess you came over to admire our masterpiece," she said, smiling in a way that displayed her dimples. "Isn't it remarkable?"

"Yes, ma'am, it is," I said in what I imagined to be a gentlemanly tone. "Real remarkable." I gazed at the house.

"Your sister Teresa . . . what a sweetie she is . . . thinks we'll win the contest hands down," Mrs. Stoneworth said. "Now, what is your opinion?"

"It's a shoo-in," I said, "Looks like your painters have gone where no painters have gone before."

"Oh, I wish you'd tell that to my husband, Russell. He indulges me, you know, but I don't think he has a real appreciation for what's being done to the house."

Colleen yanked at me. "Come see what I painted."

"Not now. Later, maybe. I've got to get back."

"It's been a pleasure meeting you," Mrs. Stoneworth said, flashing her dimples again. "I've met your parents, and of course little Colleen here, and your lovely sister Teresa. I suppose now that you're back on the happy road to recovery your folks will begin to enter the social life of Leesville?"

"I don't know." Guiltily I remembered I hadn't even asked Mom and Dad about the party last night. "They're still settling in."

Mrs. Stoneworth walked with me out to the sidewalk. Stooping to pick up a circular that had been thrown on the grass, she said, "I noticed that peculiar woman . . . Mrs. Winger . . . going into your house yesterday."

"She's going to make some drapes for our living room."

"Is she? Oh well, I guess she sews well enough. But . . ."

"But what?"

"Oh. Oh nothing," Mrs. Stoneworth said. "I guess she's all right. Just as long as she doesn't drag that oddball sister of hers to our doorstep. As for the child . . . that strange, strange child. I am so relieved she is no longer a contaminating influence on the children around here."

My stomach tightened. "What child is that, Mrs. Stoneworth?"

"Sarah Eliza . . . Elizabeth, whatever. Everyone breathed a sigh of relief when that girl was taken away."

Could she mean *Flora*? "Taken away how?" I asked.

"Oh, darlin', don't ask me. No one cares how or why. It's just a merciful blessing the girl is gone. Let us hope for good."

Your hope is in vain, I thought, reasoning that the girl had to be Flora. But why the change of name?

It was just one more confusing element, I thought, as I went home. I really hoped the mystery girl would show up again. Soon. And stick around long enough to give some answers.

◆

That afternoon I drove over to the Wingers' with Mom. If I had hoped to meet up with Flora there, or at least get a look inside the house where she lived, I was disappointed. We had barely pulled up in the driveway behind a pickup truck when Mrs. Winger came bursting out of her front door.

The two-story house had a look of neglect. Its paint was peeling and the front porch sagged. I looked up to the second floor, hoping to see a face at a window, but the panes were blank.

Without any kind of greeting, Mrs. Winger went to Mom's side of the car and asked, "You've brought the material?"

"Yes, it's there on the back seat. I'll—"

Before Mom could even get out, Mrs. Winger opened the back door and grasped the bundle. "I'll let you know when the drapes are all done," she said. "Good day to you." And, carrying the big package, she went back to the house.

I looked at Mom and laughed at the expression on her face. "Is this a good example of southern hospitality?" I asked.

"My word." Mom backed out of the driveway. "I know the woman isn't exactly talkative, but . . ."

"Maybe her house is a mess," I said, "and she didn't want us going inside. Women are like that."

Mom smiled. "Whatever." She drove down the dirt road and then onto the street. There were no houses nearby, just scrubby-looking lots. "As long as Mrs. Winger does good work on the draperies it doesn't matter to me what her home looks like."

That reminded me of the party Mom and Dad had gone to. "What kind of place does Dad's boss live in? A colonial mansion, with pillars?"

"No, Jon, the Hamptons aren't reliving *Gone With the Wind*. Their house is nice . . . fancy but not too fancy. We met some pleasant people. There was one couple in particular . . ." She went on telling what they were like and I was half listening but also thinking it was about time Mom and Dad had a social life again. Up to now their stay in the new town had been pretty dreary, thanks in part to my being sick. Well, at least that was history, I hoped.

Mom apologized for having errands to do instead of being free to show me the really interesting places in town, but I told her there'd be time for all that. It was enough just to see stores and strangers for a change.

The sights around town could wait. The only sights I wanted to see were Flora and her cat. I'd gotten only a fleeting impression of the girl before she disappeared. She looked to be around eleven or twelve, but talked like someone older.

Hey, I told myself, *forget her. She's probably just an ordinary kid.* But even as I thought the words, I knew they weren't true. Flora was someone special . . . I felt it. And I couldn't wait until we met again.

◆

Dinner that night seemed to go on forever. Teresa grandly offered to do the cleaning up, now that the dishwasher had been repaired. The rest of us sat around in the living room, talking.

After a while I yawned, announced I was really beat, and headed upstairs to bed. Instead of changing my clothes, I lay on the bed fully dressed. I read, listened to some tapes, and waited for everyone to settle down for the night.

Every time I'd hear someone in the family stirring—going down the hall, talking—I'd say silently,

Go to bed. Turn out the lights. Conk out. Please. I didn't think there was any hope of Flora showing up while people were moving about in our house.

Finally it was dark, and quiet. I waited.

It wasn't too long. I heard a rustling of leaves and I stuck my head out of the window. In just a few seconds, Flora swung onto the porch roof. She didn't make a sound. Later on I was to notice that she wore light little slippers, almost like ballet shoes but fastened with straps instead of ribbons.

She crept over to the window. "Is everyone asleep?" she whispered.

"I'm not sure," I whispered back.

"Then you'd better come down," she said, turning back to the tree.

"Wait!"

She turned.

"I'm not quite . . . I mean, I guess I could get down, but . . . I'm not sure . . ." And then I added, "I've been pretty sick."

She looked at me through the tree and leaf shadows. "Then you'd better go down the passage."

"The what?"

"You haven't noticed? It's in your closet."

"What is?"

She breathed the tiniest of sighs. "The secret passage. I used to use it sometimes. It's incredible you haven't discovered it."

I started to repeat that I'd been sick in bed all this time, but I didn't want to sound like a drag. Besides, what was she saying? Maybe Flora actually was a little crazy.

"Show me the secret passage," I said.

Without a word, she shoved the screen a little higher and crawled through the window. She started toward my closet, then turned around. "Well," she said, "come on."

I followed. It was a big closet, with my clothes, mostly unworn so far, jammed along the rod in front of the door. Farther to the right were boxes on the shelves and big boxes on the floor, where the moving men had put them.

"Oh, well, it's no wonder," Flora said, pulling on the light cord. "All this junk stacked around." She leaned over and shoved one of the boxes aside. Her voice was a little muffled. "It's over here."

I carefully closed the closet door and whispered, "What's over there?"

"The trapdoor. You'd better get a flashlight."

I did as ordered. Pushing my clothes aside, I played the beam toward Flora. There was a sort of brass ring on the floor. Before I could move closer, Flora had taken hold of it. A door lifted up from the floor.

"There, you see? It's quite simple, actually, to come and go," Flora said. "Please hold the light for me."

I moved closer to her, beyond the box she had shoved aside, and beamed the light down into the darkness. It was pitch black below and there was a ladder, not a stairway. It seemed to go straight down.

"Well, come on," Flora whispered, "shine the light for me. I can't see, you know."

I did, and she started to descend, then stopped. "Are you coming along or not?"

"Sure." I thought of going back to lock my bedroom door but decided it wasn't necessary. Holding the light with one hand, I took hold of the ladder with the other. My arm started trembling. How far did this ladder go? I had no idea.

"Wait, now," Flora commanded. "Shine the light down here. This is tricky. I have to get over to one side . . ."

I looked down to see Flora carefully propping one hand against the wall while lifting with the other. Still another trapdoor!

Then she went down again and I followed. Suddenly there was the slightest thud and Flora said, "All right, we're here."

"Where?" I asked.

"In the basement, of course. Haven't you been down here? Or wondered why a ladder is against that wall?"

"No to both," I said.

"All right, come along." She impatiently took the flashlight from my hand and I followed her and the beam across the room to a door.

Flora opened it. The hinges squeaked and night air rushed in.

"You really ought to oil those hinges," Flora said, sounding like an adult again.

"It's just a couple of steps up." She held the light for me. "And now here we are, right under your window. It's actually easier to climb the tree, but that's not always possible."

After a bit, still breathing heavily, I asked, "How did you know about the . . ." It wasn't exactly a passage. Just a drop down two floors, using ladders.

"The secret way? By wandering through the house. It was empty, you know, for quite a while. Except for Cat and me."

"But how does it go through . . . I guess . . . our dining room?"

"Take a look next time. There are built-in cupboards but a bare wall in between the two of them.

It covers the hollow place where we went down on the ladder."

The brothers who built this house, I thought. *This obviously was their inside fire escape, although not a very convenient one.*

"You have to be careful when you get to that point," Flora continued, brushing off her skirt, "because there's not much room for your feet when you lift the trapdoor. It would be easy to go plunging right on down into the basement. You could break all your bones and just lie there and rot away before anyone found your remains."

"What a cheerful thought." And what gruesome words, from a girl who looked so light and airy.

"Oh, you'd be safe, with people all around you," Flora said, starting now toward the front of our house. "But remember, I was there all alone. No one knew except for my mother and Aunt Evangeline, and they never came to the house. I always sneaked back to them while it was still good and dark."

We were at the edge of the meadow. Flora walked into it and I followed.

Something was missing, and then I realized what it was. "Where's your cat?"

"He went off somewhere. He likes to explore at night."

Then Flora hadn't come to my room to get him. Why had she appeared? *Well,* I thought, *I might as well ask.* "Was there some special reason you came over?" We had stopped whispering by now, but still I kept my voice down.

"Must there be a reason?" She turned toward me and part of her face was in moon shadow. Her hair seemed so light in the faint breeze that individual strands lifted and shone with an almost incandescent gleam.

I managed to stammer, "No reason, no . . ." while wondering if I was actually dreaming and she was some kind of woodland nymph. Even her dress looked light and airy. "How did you get the name Flora?" I asked, remembering that Mrs. Stoneworth had called her something else. *If this was the same girl.*

"I gave myself the name. I am not a Sarah Elizabeth, no matter what *he* says. Of course, Mother and Aunt Evangeline understand perfectly and call me Flora."

So she *was* the same girl Mrs. Stoneworth had talked about. But a "contaminating influence"? How could she say that? This girl was . . . I don't know what. Unpredictable? Mystifying? That and more.

Suddenly a streak of white flashed toward us from some undergrowth. "Why, here's Katmandu come back! Cat, Cat, where have you been?"

The cat gave a flying leap into Flora's arms. She held it and whispered something I couldn't hear.

"What did you call him? Katmandu?" And then I realized she hadn't been calling him Cat as in *cat,* but Kat, short for Katmandu. "How come you named him after a town in Nepal?" I asked.

"You know the place?" Now her face, fully in the moonlight, glowed with interest.

"Well, only from reading *National Geographic*. Actually, all I know is that Katmandu is in the Himalaya Mountains, where Mount Everest is located." I was about to go on about the conquering of that mountain peak but I didn't want to sound like an encyclopedia.

"Have you ever been there?" I asked instead. It's not a question I'd ask most people, but Flora was not like most people. At that moment she could have said anything and I would have believed her.

"I haven't been there yet," she said, releasing Kat and strolling on. I noticed he wasn't wearing a floral wreath tonight. "Aunt Evangeline was there, though, and had some mystic encounters. She would like to return, but that doesn't seem very likely at present."

We had gone farther than halfway across the meadow. I thought I could see the outline of her house in the distance. Flora stopped at a clearing half circled by trees. "There it is, the place," she said.

I looked. All I could see was scraggly grass.

"You don't feel the vibrations?" she asked.

"Uh . . ." I wanted to say the right thing, but still . . . "Not really," I admitted.

"It's your first time," Flora said. "The feeling will

grow if you have a receptive spirit, and I believe you do."

I couldn't help picturing a satellite dish, but I knew this was not what my companion had in mind.

"The dew will be rising," she said. "You'd better go back now. I'll stay awhile until the oneness occurs. Then I will know to continue the preparations."

She could have been talking Chinese for all the sense this was making. I felt different . . . unsure . . . mesmerized. I didn't want to leave. Yet I knew I must. I had suddenly become an outsider with a nonreceptive spirit.

Flora was drifting around the clearing as though propelled by wind. She acted as if I wasn't there anymore. Reluctantly I left, but I knew that I would return. When?

Whenever this strange girl summoned me.

NINE

I took the easy way back to my room, through the basement door and then up the stairs to the first floor. I paused in the front hallway to hear if anyone was around. All was quiet. Then cautiously I went upstairs to my room.

It took me a long time to fall asleep, and when I did, I dreamed of mountain climbing, with a white cat as guide. But the cat kept blending in with the snow, and then I'd get lost.

When I woke up, sunlight was streaming into the room and a little breeze was making the leaf patterns on the floor leap in a frenzied way. If I stared at them long enough, I could probably hypnotize myself. But wasn't I hypnotized already?

Last night. Had that really happened? Had I gone out to the meadow with Flora and heard her say all those strange things? Was there something mystical about the meadow?

And then I remembered something even more strange . . . the descent through the house on a hidden ladder in a secret passageway. Could I have dreamed that? Was I losing my grip on reality? Could it be that my brain had in fact been damaged by the fever, as my sweet little sister had suggested?

I jumped out of bed, almost taking a tumble when my foot got caught in a twisted sheet, and went over to the closet. Sure enough, big boxes full of sports gear had been shoved over in front of the door. I leaned a hand against the wall of the closet and stretched to look into the far end. It was empty. And there on the floor was the outline of a trapdoor, with a brass ring for lifting it.

I could feel my heart thumping. This was no dream. I'd actually gone out to the meadow in the middle of night with an otherworldly kind of kid. And I knew, given the chance, I'd go again.

I shoved the box back over the trapdoor. It was surprising that no one seemed to know it was there. But then Dad probably hadn't checked out every detail of the house when he bought it. And I'm sure the moving men simply shoved boxes to the places they were labeled to go. But hadn't Mrs. Tennyson, while cleaning up, noticed the door? Maybe she had, but paid no particular attention. She didn't seem to be the inquisitive type.

I closed the closet door and went back to sit on the side of my bed. It was time for me to take my temperature. Today it was probably above normal again.

As I sat waiting with the thermometer in my mouth I began wondering about the ladder in plain sight in the basement. When I had a chance I'd slip down and see what it looked like in the daytime. Ordinary, probably.

As I'd expected, my temperature was slightly elevated. But I didn't offer that information to Mom when she paused in the doorway.

"Everything normal?" she asked.

Normal? Nothing is normal. "I feel great." Mom took that as a yes and said breakfast was ready.

As we finished eating, Mom asked if I wanted to ride along when she did some errands and see a little more of the town.

"Is there all that much to see?"

"It's small, but it has charm. The downtown section is really quite nice. So far there are no malls for miles around."

"As though that's some kind of advantage," Teresa grumbled.

"How's the fast-food place?" I asked her. "Just like the ones back home?"

"Of course, it's a chain. Even the smell's the same. I'll never get it out of my hair."

"Always griping," I commented. "At least you have your health." I pretended to cough pitifully into my napkin.

"Oh, please," my sister said. "Enough pathos. Face it, Jon, your days of pampering and pity are almost over."

I turned to Colleen. "She was once an angel of mercy, but now her heart is stone."

Colleen merely looked at me over the rim of the bowl as she slurped up the milk from her cereal.

♦

The town actually did have what Mom called charm. I liked the little stores and the people who seemed really friendly when they said, "Now you all come back, hear?" instead of that trite up-North thing, "Have a good day."

"What're all those green vines growing over there?" I asked, pointing.

"Wisteria," Mom said. "Isn't it lovely?"

I didn't know about the looks so much, but I liked the sound of the word. *Wisteria.* Why did it remind me of Flora? Was it *wist* . . . mist? Or *teria* . . . mysteria?

I couldn't stop thinking about Flora. When we got home I dragged out old copies of the *Geographic.* I looked at the table of contents in issue after issue, searching for that article I'd once read about Katmandu in Nepal. Maybe it would help to explain the place's attraction for Flora's aunt and herself.

Just as I found the article, a man came to deliver and install the new curtain rods for the living room. Mom showed him where to place them and then went back to another project in the kitchen.

Colleen offered to help the man. He smilingly said he could use some help but she'd have to grow some first. I volunteered, and in about a half hour the rods were all in place.

Welford—he told us to call him that—asked if the curtains were ready. "I could put them up for you, long as I'm here."

"Mommm!" Colleen bellowed. "Are the curtains done?"

Mom came into the room and gave my sister a look. It was the look that used to make me realize I'd been impolite. But it didn't seem to faze Colleen.

"All finished with the rods?" Mom asked Welford. "They look nice."

"Yes, ma'am. I could put up the drapes, too, if you have them handy."

"I'm afraid they're not ready," Mom said.

Colleen piped up, "The crazy girl's mother is making them. Right, Mom?"

Mother gave my sister another look. This one definitely said, *We're going to have a talk later.*

"If she means the little Winger girl," Welford said, gathering up his tools, "why, I don't think she was crazy. Just different. Pretty little thing. Gone now, but not too happy about goin' is what I heard."

I was dying to say, "She's back," but of course I wouldn't. "Where'd she go?" I asked Welford in what I hoped was an indifferent tone.

"Folks say her daddy came here and got the girl and took her up North. I guess the law was on his side, but it sure does seem a pity to take a girl away from her mama like that."

"Yes, well, that is too bad," my mother said. She felt sympathetic, I could tell, but at the same time she isn't a gossip. "If you have the bill, I'll pay you now, Mr. . . . ?"

"Just call me Welford. Everybody does. We'll send you the bill, and you just take your time in paying it."

My mother was startled, and so was I. We'd never heard words like that back home.

Colleen scooted out of the house just ahead of Welford. I guess she wanted to put off the lecture she deserved.

Mom went back to the kitchen, and while the coast was clear I sneaked down to the basement to check out that ladder. Because I knew why it was there, it practically jumped out at me. But I guess to anyone not in the know, it was just a ladder hanging on a wall.

Glancing up, I could see the faint outline of the trapdoor on the ceiling. I'd never have noticed it if I hadn't made a point of looking.

I went back upstairs, picked up the magazine I'd set aside, and went out to the swing on the front porch to read it. There were lots of pictures taken in the center of Katmandu. Goats were running around among people in brightly colored clothes. The women wore lots of makeup, especially around their eyes. Even the little girls had eye marks, and some had red dots on their forehead and red lines in the partings of their hair.

I studied all the photos and several times began to read the article. But the face of Flora kept appearing in my mind. With her frail and pale looks she seemed to have nothing in common with the exotic people of Nepal. But there had to be some kind of connection. What was it? Spiritual? Mystical?

For the second time that day I told myself to get a grip. Flora was simply a young girl with an over-blown imagination. Not to mention an odd-eyed cat. A cat that sometimes wore a wreath of flowers.

Another part of the puzzle had fallen into place this afternoon. But when had her father taken her away from her mother? How had she managed to get back? Obviously she'd hidden in my room, but where did she hide out now? At her mother's house?

For whatever reason, Flora seemed to trust me. Was it because her cat . . . Katmandu . . . trusted me?

It was all so very strange.

I looked at my watch. Five o'clock. That meant seven or eight hours would have to drag by before I'd see the pair of them again.

It didn't even occur to me to go looking for Flora at her house across the meadow. Somehow I knew that our meetings could only take place at night, with the moon our only witness. If I made any attempt to change that, I sensed Flora and Katmandu would vanish from my life forever.

♦ ♦ ♦

*W*ouldn't you know. That night some people from the church stopped by to welcome my family and ask us to join the congregation, and they stayed and stayed. Even after they left, my parents sat around, talking.

Finally I looked at my watch, said, "Wow, it's late," and stood up, thinking my parents would also get up. Instead, they said, "Good night, Jon," and went on talking.

Although it wasn't my intention, I must have fallen asleep fairly fast. The next thing I knew, it was morning and Mrs. Tennyson was knocking on my bedroom door. When I told her to come in she apologized for waking me up.

"I was awake," I lied.

"I'm changing all the linens this morning because I want to get outside and wash the windows later on," she said.

"Fine. No problem." I got my robe and was heading out of the room when I heard Mrs. T. say, "Well, that's an odd thing."

"What is?" I turned and saw white hairs floating above my bed, where the cleaning woman had shaken the bedspread. My heart gave a lurch. *Kat must have been in my room last night and I was too deeply asleep to know.* "What is that stuff?" I managed to ask.

"Lordy, I don't know." Mrs. Tennyson didn't seem to care much, either, as she went on changing the bed. Her indifference relieved me. "You aren't going to wash the upstairs windows from outside, are you?" I asked, . . . a little diversionary tactic.

"Sugar, I can't," she said. "Ladders make me dizzy."

I was glad of that. She'd obviously never gone down *my* ladder. I assumed the folks would hire someone else to do the upstairs windows.

So Kat had been in my room last night. Somehow that made me feel good. It meant he wanted to be near me. I doubted that Flora had come by. If she'd called out to me, I was pretty sure I would have heard her. I edged over and pulled down the screen. This had become a daily ritual, pulling the screen up at night and shoving it down in the morning.

◆

That night I lifted the screen again and forced myself to stay awake. Sure enough, there came the pattering of paws and the soft bounce as Kat landed on my bed.

"Do you like it here?" I whispered. "Or did you come just to see me?" I smoothed his fur and he began to purr. When I settled back on the pillow he moved over to my shoulder and curled up there. The purring sound he made was so peaceful. I'd had a dog once when I was a kid but we'd never had a cat. Now I knew what I'd been missing. Of course, Kat was no ordinary creature—and I wasn't thinking of his odd eyes or the flower wreath he sometimes wore. He was just a great cat.

The next night I waited as usual, but this time neither Kat nor Flora appeared. I had to find out what was happening with them. After pulling on my clothes and grabbing the flashlight, I went into the closet, opened the trapdoor, and started down the ladder. I felt shaky, but took my time. It was harder to lift the second trapdoor but I managed. In the basement I paused to catch my breath and calm down a little, and then I went outside.

The moon was bright enough that I didn't need the flashlight as I walked into the meadow.

I'd almost reached the clearing that Flora had pointed out before when I saw a figure. Then it disappeared. When I got closer I saw it was Flora swirling around in some kind of dance. She looked like a nymph . . . the kind you see in old paintings.

Holding her arms above her head, Flora made an arc. Her head was tilted back, her hair billowing around her. She was so caught up in the dance that she didn't notice me standing there. I frankly didn't know whether to stay or to leave her to perform her ritual, if that's what it was.

Finally, whatever inner music she was dancing to must have ended, because she came to a stop. Her arms slowly lowered outward and then dropped to her sides. Her head tilted forward until it was bowed. She stood there motionless, like a flower rooted to the ground.

This was too weird. I was still wondering what to do when Flora suddenly came to life, took a deep breath of the night air, and strolled over to me.

"Do you notice a difference?" she said, by way of greeting.

"Uh . . . in what?"

"My face, my being," she said.

I just stared at her.

"If you breathe in properly when the moon is right, moonglow enters your body and you become otherworldly." She looked up at the night sky. "Just for a few moments, of course, until the beams dissipate. Perhaps it has already happened. Sad that it should be so fleeting, don't you agree?"

"Yeah, sure," I said, staring at her. She did seem to have a glow about her, but I'd noticed that the other night. I'd thought her translucent skin and filament hair just picked up night light. I didn't know the glow came from within. If indeed it did.

"I noticed you dancing," I said. Talk about stating the obvious.

"It's in preparation for the summer solstice," she said. "Much must be done before then."

"I thought the summer solstice was just something

that happened around the twentieth or twenty-first of June. Why do you have to prepare for it?"

"Because," Flora said, "I'm a druid."

"A what?"

"Surely you've heard of druids?"

"Well, not recently," I said. How lame. "I've forgotten. Are they members of a race or religion or what?"

"Oh dear," Flora said. "You really don't know, do you? Well, I haven't time to go into it now."

"It's not that late," I pointed out. "But then, I guess you have other things to do."

"Many things," she said. "And heavy work lies ahead."

She started walking away from me, but I caught up.

"You want me to help?" I don't know what had come over me. I mean, here I was in a meadow, past midnight, offering to be part of some obscure ritual. Me, Jon, a regular guy who used to shoot baskets and play field hockey. "I could help you," I repeated.

Flora stopped and gave me a long, measuring look. Finally she said, "Perhaps I will call on you when it comes closer to the time. I'll have to consult with Aunt Evangeline, however."

Aunt Evangeline. The flaky one. It figured.

"I wonder where Kat has gone. Kat, Kat," Flora called.

"Have you had Katmandu since he was a kitten?" I asked.

"No. He just came to me one day."

"What do you mean, 'came to you'?"

"Only that. He appeared."

"So . . . you don't know if you actually own him?"

Flora gave me a chiding look. "People cannot possess cats."

"But . . ."

"They're free spirits."

Like you, I thought.

Flora abruptly turned and walked away from me toward her house beyond the far edge of the meadow. Suddenly the cat streaked out from behind some trees. Flora seemed to take no notice of him as he followed along behind her. Just as she'd taken no notice of me when she'd suddenly decided to leave.

I felt like a real jerk, standing there, staring after the two of them until they faded into the shadow of the trees and were gone.

What's with you? I said to myself. *Have you become so pathetic that you'll willingly walk out to a deserted meadow in the middle of the night and be taken in by the rantings of some schizo kid who imagines she's a . . . druid?*

As I went back through the meadow toward my house I told myself that this was it. The girl was obviously certifiable. I wanted no part of her moonbeam hallucinations or plans for honoring the summer solstice. I didn't need that. I was still recovering from a sickness that had already given me enough hallucinations for a lifetime.

Back in bed, I couldn't help wondering what Eddie would say if I called and told him about this girl I'd met, and her cat. I knew what he'd say. He'd tell me I was schizzy, too—permanently out to lunch. He'd say I was making it up.

But I'd seen her dancing in the meadow, this girl who called herself a druid and claimed moonglow entered her being.

The last thought I remember before I drifted off to sleep was *How soon will I see her again?*

*I*t rained off and on for the next three days, and sometimes during the night.

Even though the humidity was high, the painters came to do our living room. Mother wanted the walls freshened up with a lighter color before the draperies were finished and hung.

Having nothing better to do, I sat on the lower step of the stairway and watched the guys with their rollers. There was a kid helping them who looked about my age. The men called him Bud.

I felt a little embarrassed, sitting there doing nothing while Bud went around with masking tape, binding the edges of all the windows and doorways.

Colleen, buttinsky that she is, had to hang around and make a nuisance of herself.

"Why are you putting tape there?" she asked the kid.

He gave her a serious look. "To keep the walls from falling down," he said.

Colleen eyed him. I could almost hear the little

wheels going around in her head. "Why would they fall down?" she finally asked.

"Well," Bud said, "it's lead-based paint, and you know how heavy lead is . . ." He winked at me, maybe because he guessed I also knew no one used lead-based paint anymore.

Colleen didn't have a clue, so she just nodded away.

"So when you put a fresh coat of lead-based paint over all the others that are on there, the sheer weight of it could make these old walls fall in a heap, right here where you're standing now."

Colleen stared at him, then nervously ran her eyes over the walls. When laughter erupted from the other painters, Colleen realized she'd been had. Her face flushed, and she crossed her arms and tried to wither the painters with a look. But since they weren't watching, she had to settle for stomping from the room.

I stood and tried to take her arm, but she shrugged free and went out through the front door, taking care to slam the screen door behind her.

The kid, Bud, took a step into the hall. "Gee, I was just kiddin' around," he said to me. "I didn't mean to upset her."

"Don't worry about it," I said. "My sister has a short fuse. But she also has a short memory. She'll be back."

"You're new here, aren't you?" the guy said.

"Yeah, we're from up North." I hated to make a

thing about my illness, but still I didn't want this kid to think I was a lazy slob. "I've been sick since before we moved, but one of these days . . ."

"Hey, you look fine." He wiped his palm on his white painter's pants and held out his hand. "My name's Homer Junior, but everyone calls me Bud."

"Jon," I said, shaking his hand.

He was a little shorter than I was, but then I'm tall for my age. His eyes were a deep hazel brown with sparkles in them, and his cheeks had rosy circles that he probably wished he could get rid of.

"I've gotta say you don't *look* sick," Bud said.

"I know. It'd be better, maybe, if I'd broken my leg."

Bud laughed. "You've got that right. I had a case of appendicitis one time and like to have died because my mom thought I was just fixin' to take a day off from school. Sometimes it seems like you have to keel right over before folks'll believe you're sick."

"Hey, Bud, you going to stand there jawin' all day or are you gonna give us some help, boy?" The skinnier of the two painters went on, "I need to have that fireplace taped before I get over there, and that won't be but a few minutes."

"Yes, master," Bud said, giving me a sideways smile. "I'm all but doin' it." Then he added, "That's my daddy, tryin' his best to work me to death."

I wished I could talk to Bud some more. He was the first kid I'd met here and in a way he reminded me of Eddie, only he seemed to have a more open nature. Eddie was friendly, but he had to know you before he reached out.

Just as I was wondering if it would be okay for me to go over and talk while Bud was taping, there was a knock at the front screen door.

I saw it was Lorraine Stoneworth from across the street and went to let her in.

"Would your mama mind if I had a few words with the painters?" she asked. "I promise not to interrupt."

I shrugged, and she stepped across the drop cloth to where Bud's dad was painting.

"Hello, Homer," she said. "You remember me? I'm Mrs. Stoneworth. We had a conversation about painting my house?"

"I remember," he said. He kept on with the brush.

"Now I know we didn't see eye to eye about how I wanted the job done." She paused, but getting no response went on, "And I can respect your feelings. But now I've come to ask a favor of you." She patted her hair nervously. "It's beginning to look like we might not get the house all painted before the judges come around to cast their critical eyes on it."

"What was the favor you wanted of me?" the painter asked.

"I was wondering if you could come on over and help them finish," Mrs. Stoneworth said. "I'd pay double. I surely would."

Homer stopped, looked through the window at the house across the street, and scratched his head. Then he turned to his partner.

"What do you think, Billy Ray? Could we give the lady a hand?"

"Looks like we could. Provided it stops raining sometime this year."

"Oh, thank you!" For a moment I thought Mrs. Stoneworth was going to give Homer a hug.

Mom came downstairs then and the two women walked out to the front porch, talking. After Mrs. Stoneworth left, Mom told me lunch was ready. Then she asked the painters if they weren't going to take a noon break.

"We sure are, ma'am," Homer said. "Just as soon as we finish this one little section."

The sun suddenly came out while we were eating. When I went back to the living room the men were sitting on the floor, having their lunch.

I sat on the lowest stair step and Bud came over, carrying a sandwich, and sat down beside me.

"So how do you like livin' here?" he asked.

"So far I haven't done anything, haven't met any-one." A vision of Flora floated in my mind but I wiped it out.

"They're some good guys around. You'll like 'em. They're real friendly, even to northerners." He gave me a little nudge with his elbow. "Want me to show you around?"

"Sure."

"You've probably got your own car."

"Me? I'm not even old enough to get a license."

"Shoot, you must be fifteen. That's when you get started down here."

I hated to admit it but I said, "I'm only fourteen."

"Go on! Sure enough?"

I nodded.

"Well, so am I. Shake." We shook hands. "Do you have a bike?"

"Yeah . . . I had one. I assume it got moved."

"All right, then, you can bike over to my house. It's not more'n a few miles."

I could almost feel the fever come back, just thinking of riding a bike that far. I doubted I could make it to the corner.

"Uh . . . when I'm feeling better," I mumbled.

Bud paused a moment before saying, "Sure," and I wondered if he thought I was just putting him off.

Mom came toward the stairs. "Honey," she said to me, "do you still want to go to the library?"

I hated having her call me *honey* in front of Bud, although he pretended not to notice. "Yeah, I guess so," I said, getting up.

"Mom, this is Bud . . ." And to him, "I didn't get your last name."

"Atkins. Pleased to meet you, ma'am," Bud said. "We sure do welcome you here, and hope you like our town."

"Why, thank you," Mom said. "So far we like it just fine."

Bud glanced over at the painters, saw they were back at work, and said, "I'd best get going before my daddy gets riled up and puts out my lights." He grinned. "Or at least turns them to low."

"Yeah, he looks mean as a snake," I said.

"You got that right." Bud clapped his dad on the shoulder as he passed him, then turned to wink at me.

♦

Mom dropped me off at the library while she went on a few errands. I had vaguely told her I wanted to do some research, which was true. Now, though, as I walked up the steps to the brick building in the brilliant daylight, fresh from talking to a normal guy like Bud, the thought of druids seemed almost laughable. And Flora . . . well, I must have been off my hinges when I followed her out to the meadow and listened to her gabble about mystic rites and moonbeams.

Inside the library it was cool and welcoming. Instead of a fluorescent glare there were pools of light coming from green-shaded lamps on long wooden tables. It was really peaceful compared to the razzmatazz public library back home, huge and computerized to the max.

I decided that as long as I was here I might as well look up druids. Then I'd go check out the SF section.

The reference books looked as though they'd been

on the shelves since time began, but they served my purpose. Druids, it seemed, had been around a long time, too.

I found out that the druids (sometimes capitalized, sometimes not) were mostly Celts who lived in Gaul, Britain, and Ireland ages ago. They were educated, in their own way, and had a lot of tribal rules. If anyone got out of line he or she was barred from the sacrificial ceremonies. This was like a low blow. I guess you could compare it to being kicked out of a baseball league, but it was even worse for those druids, being kicked out of the cult.

It seemed they held their ceremonies in oak groves. *Are those oak trees out in the meadow where Flora danced,* I wondered, *or was Flora making do with whatever trees happened to be there?*

One book said that some people believed the druids constructed the various standing circles of stones found in Great Britain and used them for summer solstice ceremonies.

Wow. I wondered whether Flora knew about this and if it somehow figured in her own plans for the summer solstice fete. Nothing she did would surprise me, but constructing a replica of Stonehenge would be beyond even her powers. So I could deep-six that idea.

I'd about had it with druids. I slammed several books shut and reached for the last one. Just before it closed, something—some words on the page—caught my eye. I opened the book again.

I wished I hadn't. What it said was: *Some druids believed in animal sacrifice.*

A sudden thought hit me and I felt a cold chill. Wasn't it the custom—I'd read or seen this somewhere—to decorate the intended victim of a sacrifice with flowers?

Katmandu . . . Kat . . . that wreath of flowers around his neck! I had never asked Flora why he was wearing it. Could it be that she was preparing him . . . getting him used to wearing the flowers? So that he would go along without a fuss to his possible . . . ?

I could hardly let myself think the words. *Kat—a sacrifice?*

No! Absolutely not! That would never happen. I'd go to the meadow every night if necessary. And if I found out Flora intended to do that deed . . . well, I'd find some way to save Kat.

I guess what I was actually doing was giving myself a good, solid reason for going to the meadow and seeing Flora again.

TWELVE

♦ ♦ ♦

*F*lora was waiting for me that night near the grove of trees. "You're late," she said. "Late? I didn't know I had to punch in at a certain time." I'd been lucky to get away at all. After Colleen went to bed she had an upset stomach and kept having to hurl. Each time, she screamed for Mom, and so there was lots of traffic in the upstairs hall. Finally all was quiet and I made my getaway, going down the secret ladders.

"Okay," I said to Flora. "I'm here. Now what?"

"While waiting for you, I managed to move a big stone from over there" . . . she pointed . . . "to over here by the other big stone. I could have used your help."

If she wanted to make me feel guilty, she was succeeding. That rock had to weigh at least seventy-five pounds. Still, what was the point? "Why'd you want them next to each other?" I asked.

"As a start for making the circle. Of course, we'll

need many more, but I do have a plan for getting them."

She'd lost me there. "You need more rocks? For what?"

"For Stonehenge, of course."

"Of course." Why was I not surprised? This girl, I could tell, made no small plans. "Stonehenge," I said, "druids, summer solstice, they all go together, don't they?"

"Exactly. I sensed you had an understanding, Jon. That's why I decided to weave you into our group."

"Oh? How many are in this group?" I had a fleeting vision of hundreds of druids swarming around, all dressed in long white robes.

"Just the four of us. You, me, Katmandu, and Aunt Evangeline."

Uh-oh. Aunt Evangeline, the fruitcake relative. It figured.

"Look . . ." I was about to say she could include me out of any druid-type rituals, but at that moment Flora turned toward me. The little bit of moonlight on her face made her skin seem almost luminous, like light on crushed pearls. But more than that, she suddenly looked vulnerable. In spite of her brave talk she was basically a little girl, playing make-believe. For what ultimate purpose I had no idea. But it seemed very important to her.

The fact was, she had come to me. She trusted me. I was a stranger to her and the whole town, but she had chosen me. Or was it Katmandu who had chosen me? At any rate, I felt they needed me. And I guess I needed them, too. In their strange, mysterious way they had given focus to my life.

"Did you bring a flashlight?" Flora asked.

"Yes." I smacked my hip pocket. "Right here."

"All right, then let's proceed." She started off and I followed.

"Where are we going?"

"To the cemetery."

"Cemetery?" I kind of yelped. "What for?"

"To get the rest of the stones."

"You're talking *gravestones?*" *Please say no, I thought.*

"Of course. Where else would they be, if not in the cemetery?"

"We can't go swiping stones from people's graves," I protested. "It's ghoulish. And against the law."

"Then don't," she said, walking away.

I caught up with her. "Besides, don't you want to be authentic?"

She glanced at me but kept walking. I turned on the flashlight so at least we wouldn't step into a gopher hole or whatever they had down here. "Flora, c'mon. This is crazy!"

She stopped, put her hands on her hips, and squinched her eyes at me. "Don't you ever call me crazy! You hear? And don't you call my Aunt Evangeline crazy, either!"

"Hey . . . I don't even know her."

"No one does! So what right do they have . . . ?" She flung her arms out angrily and strode on.

"I'm sorry," I said, stumbling along behind her. "I really didn't mean . . . I just meant like hey, we could get in trouble."

A little voice inside me said, *Yo, Jon. Deep trouble. So cut out while you can.* I ignored the voice.

"Don't worry," Flora said, the anger mostly gone from her voice. "We'll put the stones back before they're even missed."

"Oh, then I guess it'll be okay." What a spineless blob. What was I thinking? I wasn't thinking.

Flora called out over her shoulder, "Be careful, there's a ditch up ahead. And then a barbed-wire fence."

"Here, let me shine the light," I said, catching up with her.

The ditch sloped gradually and wasn't more than two or three feet deep. But the grass and weeds were long and tangled, and at the base the ground was still soft from the recent rains.

There were three strips of barbed wire on the fence. Flora put her foot on the lower one and pulled up the one above. "Squeeze through," she said. I did. Then I put down the flashlight and held the wires apart for her.

It really gave me the creeps, walking through the graveyard in the middle of the night. There were lots of big trees, many of them with drippy, droopy branches hanging down, their leaves trailing all over like ghostly arms. The moonlight, weak as it was tonight, didn't penetrate much, but when it did, it cast big shadows from the gravestones.

Flora seemed to know her way. I hurried to try to keep up with her rapid movement, but even with the flashlight, I'd stumble now and then over mounds of dirt that had to be graves.

"Flora!" Why was I keeping my voice so low? Obviously there was no one around to hear. "What's the big rush?"

"We have to go way over there, so I can check on something."

I couldn't see where she was pointing, but I followed along like a dog. "Is it much farther?" I asked.

"No."

I was puffing by now, and could feel the perspiration on my forehead. I wondered if I'd get a chill and be bedridden again.

"We're almost there," Flora said.

We'd reached a different-looking part of the cemetery. There weren't as many trees now. In fact, there wasn't much of anything. No big tombs, no stone angels, no granite markers.

"What's here?" I asked.

"Real old tumbledown gravestones," Flora said. "Give me the flashlight." I did, and she beamed it around. "See? There are only a few still standing. Whoever's buried here is long forgotten."

"But still . . ."

"I know what you're going to say again, Jon. They aren't authentic enough to use for our Stonehenge. I know that, but these gravestones will just have to do. They're the only things we have."

That's not what I'd intended to say at all. I'd been about to suggest we get the heck out of there.

When had it become *our* Stonehenge? The voice inside said, *Back out, stupid, while you can. Tell her you've thought it over and decided to take a hike . . . home.*

What I actually said was, "How are we supposed to transport these tombstones?"

She had the answer. "With my wagon. It's big enough to haul several. Of course, we'll have to make more than one trip."

I took a deep breath. We were about to cruise into the illicit world of vandalism. This I knew. But to Flora we were merely on a borrowing expedition.

I took the flashlight from her and played it over the nearest fallen tombstone. The name and date were almost obliterated by time and weather. Flora was right—these graves were forgotten, uncared for. Actually, what was the harm in using the stones as props for a summer solstice happening?

"When?" I asked. "When will we do the deed?" With those words I cast myself in the role of conspirator.

"Soon," Flora said. "Soon." Without another word she turned and headed back in the direction we'd come. I stared after her for a moment and then hurried to catch up with her.

Her sudden indifference toward me was a bit galling. I guess I'd expected some show of gratitude for agreeing to help her, but she was taking it for granted. "Are you surprised that I'm going to go along with you on all this?" I asked, still expecting some kind of thanks.

"No. If you weren't interested you wouldn't be here."

Thanks for nothing. "It's only," I said, "that it isn't safe for someone like you to go wandering alone in a cemetery in the dead of night."

"The dead are dead anytime of day or night. They can't hurt me."

"It's not the dead I was thinking about. It's . . ."

Up ahead there was a crashing noise in the underbrush just beyond a tree. I managed not to yell. I did, however, grab Flora's arm and would have galloped out of there if she hadn't pulled free.

"Kat, Kat," she called. "Come out here!"

To my relief, it actually was Katmandu, now streaking toward us.

"You wicked creature," Flora said, scooping up the cat. "Have you been chasing those poor mice again? Or was it frogs?"

The cat wriggled free and regained the ground. Then he began weaving against my legs.

"Kat likes you," Flora said. "He never likes people. He just tolerates Aunt Evangeline, who has never been anything but considerate of him. And as for my mother . . . she and Kat are barely on speaking terms."

I wondered how much conversation Flora's mother expected from a cat, anyway. What I said was, "Maybe Kat craves male companionship." I picked him up and he scooted around until he was draped across my shoulder. I couldn't tell which eye . . . the blue one or the amber one . . . was nearer my face.

When we reached the barbed wire, Kat gave a mighty leap off my shoulder and shot on ahead of us. I managed to squeeze through the wires without a scratch, but going through the ditch I caught my foot on some tangled vines and sprawled forward. It didn't hurt, but out in the meadow I saw there were huge grass stains on the knees of my pants. How was I going to explain them to Mom?

When we got back to the clearing where the two stones were, I told Flora I had to leave. "It's late. Or early, depending on how you look at it," I said.

"So tomorrow night?" Her face was in shadow but I knew she was checking to see if I was going to wimp out on her.

I said, "Sure," trying to keep my voice strong and steady. I didn't know if I was shivering from the thought of going back to that cemetery with larceny in mind, or from my wet shoes and the sweat around my neck.

Get used to it, I told myself. *If you haul those grave-stones for about a quarter of a mile, you won't be perspiring. You'll be sweating like a sumo wrestler.*

♦

The next afternoon I sneaked down to the basement with my rolled-up pants. I wondered how you get out grass stains. The only thing I knew was how to get out bloodstains, with cold water. But no one had been murdered here. Yet.

I happened to notice a container of bleach. That'd do it, I thought. Bleach.

I laid the pants on top of the washer and poured the liquid directly onto the stains. And then I stared as the khaki color faded out of the knees and they turned an off-white. The stains remained.

They weren't really good pants, but too good to throw away. What should I do? Just then I heard voices upstairs. I shoved the pants into the washer, tossed in some soap, and turned on the machine. Maybe some chemical thing would take place and the khaki color would drift back and equalize. Yeah, sure. Maybe this afternoon it would rain doughnuts.

I went upstairs and into the front hallway. Flora's mother was standing there, facing in my direction, talking to Mom. For a few seconds her eyes met mine. It was neither a friendly nor an unfriendly look, but it made me uncomfortable. It was as though her eyes were saying, *Oh, I know you.*

"I'm sorry," my mother was apologizing, "that you carried all those draperies over here. They must have been heavy."

"It's not all of them," Flora's mother said. "And anyway, I used the wagon."

As she was saying this, I was walking toward the front door, and sure enough, out there in the sunshine on the walk sat Flora's wagon. Seeing it spooked me. Until now, my nighttime adventures and my daytime routines were so separate I hardly let them mingle in my mind. But here was a connection—the red wagon, useful for hauling drapes and tombstones.

Mom and Flora's mother were coming toward me. I wanted to leave, but all I did was back toward the stairs.

"Can I drive you home?" Mom asked. "We could put the wagon in the trunk."

"No, no, walking's good, especially for my sister."

"Your sister?" Mom looked startled. "Why didn't you bring her inside?" She went to the screen door and opened it. "Where is she?"

"Don't bother," the woman said. Her eyes met mine and held for a moment. "Leave her be," she said.

I looked away. Had she meant me? To leave Flora alone?

Mom and Mrs. Winger walked out on the front porch and I followed. Was I going to meet Flora's eccentric aunt?

Apparently not. A figure was making its way across the meadow, already too far away to call to.

"Oh dear," Mom said. "Well, when you finish the rest of the draperies, please give me a call and I'll drive over to get them. I really don't expect door-to-door service."

Mrs. Winger gave a little nod, went down the steps, stooped for the rusty handle, and trundled the wagon down the sidewalk. The wheels squeaked.

We stood there, Mom and I, watching her go into the grassy meadow, with the other figure now far ahead.

"Strange woman," Mom murmured. "And strange sister."

"Yeah. I wonder if they're really crazy and that makes them strange, or if they're strange because people *say* they're crazy."

"Jon, I don't know." Mom turned and went into the house, and I followed. "People are so unfair. They make judgments that aren't always based on facts."

"Right," I agreed.

"And actually, who are we to say how other people should behave?"

"Right," I said again.

Mom went into the living room and picked up one of the drapes. "I can't help but wonder about the little girl," she said.

"Huh?"

Mom was holding the drape against the window,

I guess to get an idea of how it would look there. "The girl they say is gone. I wonder where she went, and why, and if she'll ever be back with her mother."

"I have a strange feeling she will," I said.

"Really?" Mom put down the curtain and laid an arm on my shoulder as we walked from the room. "You have a sensitive nature, Jon."

"Come on, Mom!" I protested.

"No, that's good. To know and care about people. You're the sort of person who would climb out on a limb to help someone."

"Actually, I'd use a ladder," I said.

Mom laughed, not guessing that I was speaking from actual experience.

THIRTEEN

♦ ♦ ♦

*T*o my great surprise, I got a letter from
Eddie that day. It wasn't much of a letter,
but then Eddie's not much of a writer.

Yo, Jon:
How come you haven't called lately?

(I haven't called because there's nothing to tell you
except what I can't tell you.)

Anything going on down there?

(There certainly is, and it'd spin your eyeballs to
know just what's going on . . . or about to.)

It's pretty dull here. Dave has gone to camp so
his pool is out of bounds. Maybe I could come
down to see you on the bus.

I'm sorry to say my first reaction was *Oh no!* The
last thing I wanted right now was to have Eddie here

in the house . . . in my room. But how could I think this? Eddie was my best friend. It wasn't his fault if he didn't know about Flora.

Let me know how you're feeling. It would be boring just hanging out like before you left and not doing anything.

(Wonderful, Eddie. So being with me when I was sick was a bore. Thanks for letting me know that.)

Anyway, just thought I'd clue you in to the fact that I'm still kicking, even if you haven't called lately. You haven't done anything stupid like dropping dead, have you? Ha ha, just kidding.
Eddie
P.S. How's Teresa? Don't tell her I asked.

I shoved the letter into my pocket. Is Eddie serious, I wondered, about coming down for a visit, or is he just hard up for something to say? I doubted that he had enough money for even a bus ride down here. I doubted, too, that his folks would bankroll the trip, though they were always glad to get him out of the house.

I would have liked to see Eddie, but not now. Not with the summer solstice coming up.

At that moment I realized just how involved I was with Flora. All day, at odd times, visions of her now occupied my mind. Flora . . . and her cat. I was linked with them in my daydreams, and at night I was drawn to the meadow where mystic rites were being planned. I didn't care if Little Miss Moonbeam was somewhat bossy. She had to be, didn't she, to get things done? She'd mesmerized me, that was for sure. Hadn't I committed myself to her, and to her ceremonies?

♦

"What do you intend to wear?" Flora asked that night as we sat in the meadow.

"Wear? When?"

"For the ritual, of course. Ordinary clothes won't do. Especially what you happen to be wearing now."

"I wouldn't wear these," I said, picking at some loose threads of my cutoffs. I'd decided that hacking the legs off the pants was the only way I could get rid of the grass stains, but the alteration hadn't been a big hit with Mom.

"Jon," she'd said. "You shouldn't have cut off those pants. They were still good. If you wanted more shorts, I would have bought you some, instead of ruining those."

"They're pathetic-looking cutoffs, anyway," Teresa had said. "It takes more to be cool than showing off your legs." And then she added, "*Your* legs, anyway. They're white and spindly. You ought to sit out in the sun and get some color so you don't look like you've crawled out from under a rock."

"Oh, sod off," I said to her. I'd read that in an

Irish story. It meant about the same as a common American expression, and I could get away with saying it out loud.

"You're supposed to do that with jeans, not pants," Colleen piped up. "And rip them and make them look worn out."

"Thanks, one and all," I said, "for your interest in my wearing apparel." Since Mom had left the room, I advised my sisters that they could *both* sod off.

Now as we sat in the meadow in the moonlight, Flora was going on about those same cutoffs—not about the shorts themselves, just that they didn't have the right look.

"What are you going to wear?" I asked.

"Aunt Evangeline is creating a gown for me. It will be layers of a gauzy material that floats and swirls with the dance. And a wreath for my hair."

"Maybe I could wear a cape that swirls out, too," I said. "My mother has a black one. Unless she got rid of it before we moved."

"Mmmm." Flora clasped her hands around her bent knees. "A black cape doesn't seem to fit the occasion. Too much like Count Dracula."

"My father has a paisley silk robe he never wears. Maybe I could sneak it out for just the one night."

"Mmmm," Flora said again. Katmandu, who had been chasing through the grass, came up to us and rubbed against me and then Flora. "You know what you'll be wearing, don't you, Kat?" Flora said.

"The wreath of flowers?" I asked.

"Exactly. Jon, I think now we should talk about the circle."

"The Stonehenge circle?"

"Yes. Actually, there should be more than one, but with all the hauling of stones . . ."

"What did you do last year?" I asked.

Flora got up. "I wasn't here last year." She began twirling around.

"Where were you?" I got up also.

"I don't know," she said vaguely. "Someplace. Cincinnati."

"What were you doing there?"

"Mostly trying to run away." Flora began walking, toe against heel. If there'd been chalk on her shoes she'd have marked a circle.

I followed along behind her.

"Running away from your mother?"

"No, silly. *Him.*"

My heart thumped a little. I stopped following, and walked beside her. "Are you saying you were kidnapped, Flora?"

"I'd call it that. The law wouldn't. He's my father and he has custody, at least most of the time. But when I was supposed to come to my mother's last summer, he wouldn't let me."

"How come?"

"Ask him." She left off making the circle and went over to lean against a tree. I joined her. "What he told me was, my mother hadn't been well and I'd be too much for her. A blatant lie."

"Didn't you write to her?"

"Yes, but I thought she wasn't writing back. The thing is, my father didn't have a mailing address, just a post-office box number, and he was the one who picked up the mail. He never gave me any of my mother's letters. So for a long time I actually did believe she was sick and didn't want me around. But after a while I got suspicious. I mean, she could at least have written to me, or asked Aunt Evangeline to write."

"Why didn't you just call her up?"

"How could I when we didn't have a phone? We have one now, but of course I never answer it. In case it's him calling."

"Your father sounds really bad. How'd he get custody in the first place?"

Flora gave a little grunt. "By telling the judge my mother was unstable and that my aunt had delusions."

She fixed her gaze on me. "You know *delusions,* don't you? It's when you think you're someone you're not. It was a terrible thing for my father to tell the judge, but I guess he believed it. Anyway, I got dragged off to Cincinnati."

"How did you manage to get away?"

Flora sighed. "It's a long, sad story, Jon. I had no friends to speak of at the school he made me go to.

But this last spring I met a woman down the street from us who had a cat."

"A cat?" *What did a cat have to do with all this,* I wondered. Flora went on to explain.

"I used to stop there after school to play with Fluffy. The woman, Elsie, was very nice and very agreeable. When I finally thought of a plan, I felt she'd be the one to help me. So one day I asked her if I could use her house as a mailing address."

It *was* a long story. And a confusing one, too.

"What I told Elsie was this: I wanted to surprise my father but I needed to get a secret letter first. It wasn't a total lie, you know. I did want to surprise him . . . by leaving."

"So then you wrote to your mother . . . ?"

"Yes, and asked her to send some money to Elsie's address. She did, and I bought a ticket on the next bus and came home."

"Wow." We began walking. "Didn't he come looking for you?"

"Naturally. But he couldn't find me. He even had the sheriff searching. There was a court order or something. Anyway, he gave up and went back to Cincinnati after a while. I guess because of his job."

"I'm surprised he didn't file a missing child report. Or did he?"

"Probably not. Because the last thing he said to my mother before he took off was, 'I know she's around here someplace, and you're going to be in trouble when that child is located.'"

"So where . . . ?" I started to ask, and then I remembered. "You were hiding out in our house . . . in my room!"

"That's right. And with the secret passage I could go there and leave, with no one the wiser. Once I made an escape when the real estate agent suddenly showed up. Kat was with me, but he was very good."

"Didn't it get boring after a while, hiding out?"

"It could have. But I made up games. And my Aunt Evangeline . . . the one people say things about . . . kept me going by thinking up adventures."

"Such as . . . ?"

Flora didn't bother to answer. We were now standing beside the two big stones that had been in the meadow already.

"Ideally we should have twenty of these and they should be about twenty-two feet high," Flora murmured.

"Good luck on that." I was hoping she'd changed her mind about the tombstones.

"But since we have to settle for a miniature version of Stonehenge, it's lucky we at least have the cemetery with its stones." Flora sighed. "The problem right now is, how are we going to mark the circle for them to stand around?"

"Flour?"

"What if it rains?" she asked.

"We could use cement, then."

"Jon, that's a wonderful idea. Where will you get it?"

Me? This was my job now? "Don't worry about it," I said.

Katmandu suddenly came streaking out from the trees, straight to me.

"Have you had Kat for a long time?"

"Yes. You can't imagine how happy he was to see me when I came back on that bus."

I picked up the cat. "Why was he wearing a flower wreath the first couple of nights he came to my room?"

"I wanted him to get used to it."

"What for?"

"For his part in the ceremony."

"And what is that?" I asked, scratching Kat under the chin.

"He's to be on the Slaughter Stone."

"What?"

"It's one of the altars, along with the Heel Stone, the Bluestones—"

"I know that," I interrupted. "But why will he be there on the . . ." I could hardly say it, "the Slaughter Stone?"

"Well, I dearly hope Kat will sit quietly before the burning oils and offer up his wreath of flowers, as I will offer up my wreath of leaves and you will . . . what sort of wreath do you imagine you should wear? Leaves also?"

"Whatever." I took a deep breath of relief. Kat

wasn't in jeopardy. "How many nights from now will all this take place?"

"Five, after tonight. Oh dear, and there's still so much to do!"

It would be a lot simpler, I thought, if everything didn't have to be done after dark. But daylight meanderings were out of the question for Flora, still in hiding. As for me . . . I shuddered to think of Colleen trailing along after me with her nonstop chattering. Or of Eddie coming down for a visit and finding out. I could imagine the smart-ass things he'd say.

". . . Aunt Evangeline is the druid authority, after all," Flora was explaining. "I'm just learning the ways."

A thought occurred to me. "What if your aunt considers me an outsider?" I said. "She might not want me to witness the rituals. I mean, aren't they sacred?"

"Very sacred. But I'll explain to Aunt Evangeline that you have proven yourself by helping with the stones and circle . . . and anything else that may come along."

I was foolishly pleased. Me, Jon Connor, pleased to be part of a mystical druid ceremony!

Flora began doing twirls. "You'd better go now," she called out. "I must be alone so I can get into the proper mood to compose my dance."

"All right," I said, feeling a little hurt, like a kid being sent from the room.

"Tomorrow night . . ." her voice trilled as she spun around.

I walked a ways and then turned back. As she danced in the moonlight in the meadow she looked more than ever like a wood nymph. If I blinked and opened my eyes again, would she be gone?

FOURTEEN

◆ ◆ ◆

*T*he next day I was in the living room reading up on Stonehenge when I was almost blinded by a flash of light. "What the . . . !"

"Don't freak out, freak," Colleen said. "I'm just trying to use up this film so I can get it developed."

"There's no law that says you have to use up the entire roll."

"But I want to. What's that big bruise on the side of your leg?"

"What?" I twisted around to look. I was wearing the cutoffs again . . . mostly to annoy my sisters. Right to the side of my knee was a huge purplish spot. Then I remembered. Coming up the ladder last night I'd hit my leg on the edge of the trapdoor. "It's nothing, I just bumped into something."

"Clumsy! I'm going to take pictures of the Painted Lady now."

"So go."

I went back to Stonehenge. *Situated in England . . .* etc., etc., etc., . . . *once thought to have been built by Celts and druid priests for druidical rites.* Hmmm. Once thought. *But it is now known that these peoples did not come to what is now known as Britain until a thousand years after Stonehenge was abandoned.* Hah. Were Flora and her aunt aware of this?

Not built by druids, huh? Then who did construct it? There were probably lots of theories floating around. Frankly, I didn't care. And I wouldn't mention it to Flora, either. Let her enjoy her pagan rites, whatever they might turn out to be.

I was back to wondering how I could lay hands on some cement when Colleen came bursting into the house again.

"Your friend wants to see you," she said.

My heart missed a beat. I almost said, "You mean Flora?" but luckily I didn't. "Who do you mean?"

"Buuuuuuuud!" Colleen said.

"*Bud?* He's out front?"

"No, he's helping to paint the house. Eric's house."

I tossed the book aside and lit out of there and across the street. I found Bud at the side of the house, painting trim on a window.

"So they've got you working on the monstrosity," I said.

"They sure have." Bud grinned. "Isn't this a putrid shade of pink?"

"Yeah. I thought your father didn't want this job."

"He doesn't. Afraid it would put him in a bad light. So he sent me over instead. I haven't got a reputation to ruin."

"It looks almost finished."

"Yes, the main part sure is done, but Mrs. Stone-worth wants some extra touches to make a big impression on the judges. She purely does want to win that contest and get herself famous."

"How long do you have?"

"She says it has to be done by the end of this week. I don't mind the work. She's paying good money and I can use it for school."

School. I hadn't thought much about school. It was still weeks away. I didn't want to think about starting in a new place and among a bunch of strangers. *Eddie.* It would be my first year in school without him. I decided to go home right then and call him, or at least answer his letter.

"Well, keep up the good work," I said to Bud. "And try not to get too nauseated."

"Hey, where you going? I want to get my picture taken with you."

"You do?" I felt a sudden mood upswing.

"Yeah, don't you want to? I sent your little sister over to ask you."

"I'll get her." I found Colleen and took her back to where Bud was painting. He was off the ladder now.

We posed with our arms around each other's shoulders.

"That surely is a good camera," Bud said. "Maybe I'll save up and get me one of those."

I stood around talking to Bud while he went back to work. It turned out we both liked the Yankees and the Blackhawks. Bud asked if I'd ever met Air Jordan up in Chicago.

"No, but I saw him play one time. It was great."

"You sure are one lucky guy," Bud said. "Saw him play. Oh lordy."

We were still going on about sports when Mom called to me from beside our car. I walked over to see what she wanted.

"I have to go shopping," she said, "and I thought you might like to ride along and pick up something for Teresa's birthday."

I'd totally forgotten about that prime event. "When is it?"

"Four days from now. Since she doesn't have any close friends here, we'll have to make it up to her by having a big family event . . ."

Mom went on talking, but my mind had braked at the words *four days from now*. The summer solstice . . . the druid ceremony!

"Is something the matter?" Mom asked.

"Huh? Oh, no. I was just thinking I should go get my wallet."

"Fine. And why don't you change those pants, too? What's that on your leg?"

"Just a bruise. I'll be right back." I called over to Bud, "See you later!" and then raced into the house.

When we got to the bakery I told Mom I'd walk down the street and look for a gift while she ordered the cake.

I passed a hardware store. *Cement!* Wow, the gods

must be looking out for me. I ducked inside and bought the smallest bag they had. It weighed a ton. Then I crossed the street to a boutique.

They had lots of girly-girly stuff there. I was the only guy in the place. I walked past the lingerie fast and went to a counter of costume jewelry. There was so much of it, how was I supposed to decide?

A woman came over and asked, "Could I show you something, sugar?" I was glad the teenage clerk was standing too far away to hear. When I said I was looking for a gift for my teenage sister, the woman made several suggestions. I finally settled on a pair of silver earrings with dolphins dangling from them. Teresa had said several times that she wanted to go to Hawaii and swim with the dolphins.

After the clerk handed me the earrings, gift-wrapped, I asked her if I could have a shopping bag. A big one. I put the package of cement into it along with the tiny box covered with curly ribbons.

Fortunately, Leesville was a town where people didn't lock their cars, so I was able to stash the shopping bag on the floor of the back seat. Mom was nowhere in sight. I leaned against the car and waited for her.

A couple of guys about my age gave me curious looks as they walked by. I wondered if all the kids here knew one another and these guys recognized me as a stranger. They might be in my class this fall. At that moment I felt like someone on an ice floe, cut off from everybody else. But there was Bud. Maybe we'd become friends and hang out together.

Again, I thought of Eddie. No one could replace him. We had such a long history together. For sure I was going to write him.

Finally Mom came back with her arms full of packages. "I ordered the cake," she said. "Strawberry. And down at the stationery store I found paper streamers and balloons and pretty flowered paper plates and napkins. Can you think of anything else?"

It sounded like a little kid's birthday party to me. I guessed that if Teresa couldn't hang out and party with her old friends up North she'd rather just sulk in her room. But I said, "Sounds good. What're you and Dad giving her?"

"A couple of outfits and some Victorian floral boxes for whatever, and some fun jewelry."

"I got her jewelry, too. Earrings."

"Oh well, she loves variety." Mom drove down a few blocks and then stopped at a pharmacy. "I have to run in and pick up your prescription," she said.

"How long do I have to take that stuff?"

"Darling, I hope not forever."

As I watched her go into the store, I thought, *I hope not forever, too.* Was I ever going to get completely well? Would I always be a semi-invalid? My sport was tennis. Dad was good at it, too, and so was Teresa. Sometimes in the evenings back home, before I got sick, we used to go out to the courts and play. Now I wouldn't even be able to volley very long. Even climbing up and down that ladder at night made me out of breath. But I knew the tree climb would be even worse, and it really wasn't safe to go through the house and down the stairs.

Mom came back with the white package. "I picked up some film for Teresa's birthday, too," she said. "I'll let you be the court photographer. You're so good with a camera."

I just hoped the party would close down before it got too late. I had other, more pressing plans for that same evening. It was lucky in a way that Flora didn't dare come out until it was good and dark.

I must have been frowning because Mom said, "What's the matter? I thought you liked taking pictures."

"I do. No problem." And then I had to keep from smiling. It had just occurred to me that I might photograph the other event . . . the ritual in the meadow, beneath the trees, in the moonlight.

For all I knew it could be the first time in the history of the world that a druid ceremony had been captured on film.

FIFTEEN

♦ ♦ ♦

*T*hat night I left the house by way of the
ladder once again. Flora was waiting for
me in the meadow and she had the wagon. Oh good
lord, she was really going to do it. *We* were really
going to do it.

"You're late again. Come along," she said, taking
hold of the handle and starting toward the cemetery.
"It's a good thing the moon's almost full tonight.
We'll be able to see."

And be seen, I thought. It crossed my mind to ask
Flora to rethink the tombstone part of the ceremony.
We were going to pretend the gravestones were
Stonehenge stones. Couldn't we go a step further
and just pretend there were stones when there
weren't any at all?

The thought crossed my mind, as I said. But I
kept my mouth shut. I guess Flora's approval meant
too much to me by then. I wanted her to think I was
an adventurous guy. And maybe I was. I'd gone

along with everything so far without a bleat, and I wanted to keep on going. I had to see this through.

We reached the ditch. It had dried out a lot, so no problem there. Then we came to the barbed-wire fence. Flora had it all figured out. She went through first, and then as I lifted the lower wire, she pulled the wagon to the other side. Then she helped me climb between the wires.

Making our way through the cemetery that night was almost more spooky than the other time. The moonlight made ghosts of the tombstones. And either there were more night sounds than before, or I was more attuned to them. Frog croaks rumbled in a chorus, and sudden scuttling noises came from the bushes. I almost panicked when an owl suddenly hooted in the tree overhead.

"Come along, Jon," Flora said, up ahead with the wagon. "There's no turning back now."

Why not? I felt like saying. *We haven't really done anything. Yet.*

In a short time we had. Flora heaved one of the fallen flat stones onto the wagon, then went to the next one.

"Here," I said. "Let me help." *Let me get totally involved in this thievery.*

Even with the two of us lifting, the stone was heavy. How had Flora been able to lift one by herself? Her fragile looks were deceptive. We piled two more gravestones onto the wagon.

"Isn't this enough?" I asked. "We could break the axle."

"One more, so we won't have to make so many trips."

It was backbreaking work, getting that wagon with its heavy load through the cemetery. We took turns pulling and pushing. The barbed-wire fence was even harder. We had to remove some of the stones and do everything twice. The wagon shot to the bottom of the ditch easily, but it was murder getting it up to the other side. I tried at one point just to carry a gravestone in my arms, but I couldn't get the momentum to walk up the bank with it.

By the time we finally got all the stones to the edge of the meadow, I was wrung out. I had to sit down for a few minutes until my breath stopped coming in gasps. My chest felt close to exploding. Flora, who had worked as hard as I, didn't seem a bit out of breath, but she sat down with me anyway.

"This next trip will be easier," she said.

"Flora," I said, still gasping a little, "I just can't do it again. Not tonight." My clothes were soaked, and I felt chilly and feverish at the same time.

She looked at me sitting there in the moonlight, my arms on my bent knees and my chest going in and out. I half expected her to dismiss me, weakling that I was. But instead, she said softly, "Tomorrow night will do as well, Jon."

I wiped my face with the tail of my T-shirt although it was damp, too. "Did I tell you," I said, when my breathing had calmed down, "I got the cement for the circle."

"You did? Oh, you are a marvel. Whatever would I do without you?"

Her words made me feel stupidly pleased. All I said was, "It wasn't that hard to get it."

After I'd helped Flora pull the wagon over to the grove and unload it, I felt so weak it took an effort just to walk home. I didn't think I could make it up the secret ladder passage so I took a chance and walked up the basement stairs. Hearing no sound, I sneaked up the rest of the way.

Upstairs, I wanted like anything to stand in the cool spray of a shower, but at two A.M.? Instead, I took my shorts and T-shirt into the bathroom, washed down, and threw the clothes I'd worn into the hamper. I hoped they wouldn't mildew before they got laundered.

◆

I didn't feel great the next morning, but still not as bad as I'd expected. My muscles were sore, but then why wouldn't they be? I hadn't done anything very physical for weeks now.

Still, I was wiped out enough to take a nap that afternoon. I suddenly woke up to the sound of voices downstairs. *We've been found out* was the first thought that went through my head. But they were soft voices coming, I could now tell, from the living room. I went down the steps, glanced outside, and nearly froze. The red, rusted wagon was on our front walk.

I saw now it was Flora's mother in with Mom. I guessed she'd brought the rest of the curtains. Had the wagon been cleaned of dirt? Well, obviously.

I slipped out to the kitchen to get a soda. When I came back, Mom was nowhere to be seen, but Mrs. Winger was standing by the front door. Our eyes met. She said nothing, so being the polite gentleman I said, "Hello, Mrs. Winger. I'm . . . uh . . . Jon."

She gave me an unblinking look which so unnerved me that I blustered, "I'm a friend of Flora's."

Unsmiling, she replied, "I don't know any Flora."

Now I was really unnerved and didn't know what to say next. (Excuse me, I must have got the name confused?) Fortunately, Mom came back with her purse and I escaped up the stairs.

For the rest of the day I felt really uneasy. I wondered if Flora's mother knew about the ceremony. Maybe she did and disapproved. Had she really been saying I shouldn't see Flora again? To me, that was now impossible. The strange girl had become a part of my life. Secret, it's true, but important all the same.

That night I went down the ladder again. I half expected to find Mrs. Winger waiting for me in the meadow, warning me not to come back there again.

To my great relief, it was Flora as usual. I told her

about what I'd said to her mother, and her mother's reply. Flora only laughed lightly. "Of course that's what she'd say. Officially I'm not here at all."

"Does she know about the summer solstice and everything?"

"Naturally. Aunt Evangeline and I talk about it a great deal, and while Mother isn't involved, she does take an interest."

"They know about me, too?"

"Yes. I tell them everything. Mother herself said, 'Flora, if you trust the boy, he must be all right.'"

"How did you know you could trust me?" I asked.

"Just a feeling. I knew Kat trusted you, too, or he wouldn't have made those trips to your room. He has great intuition." She picked up the wagon handle. "Well, Jon, shall we start now? We have to get the rest of those gravestones tonight."

Feeling strangely lighthearted, I went along with Flora. Kat accompanied us, darting away and then back again.

"I think Kat realizes we're fast approaching the ceremony," Flora said. "As I told you, he's very intuitive. I'm going to weave a very special wreath of flowers for him to sacrifice."

I almost said, "I was afraid you were going to sacrifice Kat," but I thought it just as well not to mention it.

We reached the deserted part of the cemetery at last and once again loaded gravestones onto the wagon.

Tonight, it seemed even harder than before to get the heavy wagon past the fence and through the ditch, but then my muscles were still weak from the previous night. Again, the work hardly seemed to affect Flora. Maybe her adrenalin kicked in when she needed strength.

After we unloaded the stones next to the first batch, I flopped down and did some deep breathing while Flora flitted around, practicing her dance. Kat followed her, leaping now and then as though he were doing his own little cat dance.

Finally Flora came over and dropped to the grass beside me and Kat draped himself across my knees.

"Where is the cement for the circle?" Flora asked.

"In my closet."

"Let's go get it."

"Now?"

"Time's passing," she said.

"I know, but . . ." I didn't want to say how weak I felt. I'd never told her much about my illness and this hardly seemed the time. "You're sure we need the cement now?"

"Absolutely. Come on, I'll go with you."

I thought Flora was taking a chance, walking in the open meadow in the moonlight, but she didn't seem concerned. Of course, this wasn't like strolling around a mall. There wasn't a soul in sight and all the houses were dark. All except ours, as it turned out. A pale light was coming from the living room and when I peeked in the window I saw Teresa slumped in a chair watching a late movie on television.

I sneaked back to Flora. "I'll have to go up the ladder."

"Okay, let's go."

I marveled at her courage, going into my house, but maybe she came along to see that I didn't just call it a night and hit the sack.

Flora went up ahead of me, which was good, because she opened the various trapdoors. It was all I could do, with my shaky muscles, to make it up the ladder.

When we reached the closet of my room I pulled on the light cord and dragged the bag of cement from under some old sports clothes.

"This is too heavy," Flora said. "Besides, we won't need this much. Let's pour some out." We did, into an old hockey helmet that was lying in the closet. It was really hard to keep from coughing from the cement dust in the air.

"Now, get me a pillowcase," Flora said.

I stealthily opened the closet door, grabbed a pillowcase from the bureau, and scuttled back to the closet. Flora put the bag of cement into the case. "Tie it over my wrist," she said.

I did. Even though her wrist was tiny, there wasn't much fabric to knot around it. "It might not hold," I said.

"It'll do until I get down to the ground," she said.

I was relieved to realize Flora didn't expect me to go back with her. She left the closet and made her way through my darkened room to the window, where moonlight fluttered in. She turned at the window and whispered, "Farewell, until tomorrow night."

"Yes, farewell," I whispered back. As she disappeared in the leafy tree branches, I flopped onto my bed, fully dressed. I meant to get up in a couple of minutes, but first I wanted the muscles that had taken so much punishment to loosen up a little.

Was I really up to all this? Sure I was. I pushed aside the nagging thought that Flora and I weren't home free yet, that something could happen to screw up the ceremony. Before I knew it, I fell into an exhausted sleep.

*T*he next morning I leaned against a kitchen counter and ate cold cereal while I watched Mrs. Tennyson haul out stuff from the refrigerator so she could clean it.

I thought of trying to see if Mrs. Tennyson knew anything about the situation between Flora and her father. But how could I get around to it? Aha! Sneakily . . . by way of curtains!

"How do you like the new drapes?" I asked. "That you and Mom put up in the living room?"

"Very nice," Mrs. Tennyson said, dubiously eyeing and then discarding an almost-empty jar of olives.

"Too bad about that woman's little girl . . . Mrs. Winger's," I said. "I heard the father came down and dragged her away."

"I think you got it wrong," Mrs. T. said, as I'd hoped she would. With a slight groan she got up and went to the sink, where she washed out the sponge. "The story I heard was he couldn't find her. Folks believed, though, that she was around here somewhere."

"Was he a mean guy? The father?"

"I don't think he was mean, just concerned. He didn't want his daughter raised by two daft women."

"Mrs. Winger seemed okay to me," I said, rinsing out the cereal bowl and putting it and the spoon into the dishwasher. "Not very talkative, maybe."

I wanted to hear more about the father, though. "How come he"—I almost said 'Flora's father'!—"married Mrs. Winger in the first place, if he thought she wasn't all there?"

Mrs. Tennyson gave a short laugh and looked at me. "I guess you don't know yet how blinded a young man can get by love."

I felt myself flushing a little. "Sure . . . I can understand that."

"And they say Belinda Winston was a lovely creature when she was young. Fair-haired, blue-eyed, and a complexion like melted vanilla ice cream."

Good lord, I thought, *she could be describing Flora.*

Mrs. Tennyson, her head leaning into the bottom of the refrigerator again, said, "I hear tell he's got himself a new wife."

"Flor—" I stopped myself in time. "The father, you mean?"

"Yes, some Yankee girl. I hear they both work for the government. In what capacity, I couldn't say."

This woman was a font of information. "How'd you hear all this?" I asked, straddling a kitchen stool.

"The sheriff, Luther Davis, is my first cousin, once removed. He used to know Elroy Winger when he lived here." Mrs. T., finished with the wiping up, said, "If you'd hand me those things on the table it would be a big help."

As I passed along milk, orange juice, and cheese, I tried to think of how to extract more information without arousing her suspicions. Then Mrs. Tennyson added of her own accord, "Too bad he didn't locate her . . . the girl, I mean. He's well fixed, could give her advantages."

"Money isn't everything," I said, sounding sanctimonious.

"True enough. And maybe the girl's better off in the long run with her own mother. But where she is in the meantime, no one knows."

"Just gone, I guess." I stood up. "And I'm out of here, too." I went upstairs and wrote the letter to Eddie that I'd been putting off. It was boring because the only exciting thing in my life was top secret.

On my way downstairs with the letter, I heard Teresa on the front porch, shouting something. As I reached the door, she brushed past me, sobbing.

"What's the matter?" I asked, startled.

"Oh, just leave me alone!" she yelled, racing up the stairs.

I stepped out to the porch, where Mom was standing, looking toward the house across the street.

"What's the matter with Teresa?" I asked. "Did she break a fingernail or something equally tragic?"

"She just found out that her boyfriend has been dating someone else."

"I always thought Ace was a lowlife," I said.

"Now Teresa says she wants to switch to a different university this fall so she won't run into him. But she probably wouldn't anyway . . . the enrollment's several thousand."

"Oh, she'll meet someone new." I sat down on the porch swing. "Teresa's not bad looking. And her disposition isn't always lousy."

"My goodness, you do get carried away with compliments." Mom picked some dead leaves off a potted plant. "I just hope Tess cheers up before her party. It would be nice if she'd made a friend or two here, but she says why bother when she's about to leave." She sat down on the top porch step. "I hate to think of her going so far away."

"She'll come home holidays. It's not as though she's going for good."

"Of course not," Mom said.

A strange remembrance came to me then, and I wondered if Mom was thinking of the same thing. Back when I was sick, really sick and supposedly in a coma, I heard my parents and the doctor talking in the hall outside my room. "I'm doing my best to pull him through," the doctor said, "and we've just got to believe he'll make it." I heard a little soblike sound from my mother and when she came back into my room again, I wanted to say, *I'm not going anywhere.* But I couldn't get the words out.

"We'll make it a good party for Teresa," I said now. "Just us." And I thought, *I can do this for my sister and for my parents, even if it means getting to the ceremony late.*

The phone rang and Mom went inside to get it. Back home none of us bothered to answer because it was almost always for Teresa.

I wasn't really listening but couldn't help hearing Mom say, "Oh, I'm really sorry . . . we would love to, but we're having a family birthday that night."

I wandered over to the Painted Lady to see if Bud was still working. He was, in the back, up high on a ladder.

"How's the weather up there, sailor?" I called out.

Bud twisted around and grinned down at me. "It's somewhat stultifyin'," he said. "Listen, don't go away. I'm comin' down right about now."

He did come down, with his brush and empty paint can.

"Still putrid pink," I said, looking at the can. "Must be your favorite color."

"Jon, I tell you it about makes me sick, but Mrs. Stoneworth has got herself in a frenzy about this color. She wants every window trim to have it somewhere. I have got to work my way all around the second story and I don't know how I'm going to get it done in time."

"When's the deadline for the contest?"

"I couldn't tell you that. But I know the judges will be around soon. Maybe in two or three days."

The back door opened and Lorraine Stoneworth came out, wearing a purple sun outfit and flip-flops with artificial grapes on them.

"Bud, is there some problem?" she asked. Meaning, *Why are you standing there, not working?*

"No problem, ma'am," Bud said. "I just came down to get more paint and to move the ladder."

"At the rate it's going, I wonder if it will be done in two days," Mrs. Stoneworth said.

"It takes climbing time, working high up," Bud said as he sloshed paint from a large bucket into the smaller one. "And I'm working with a brush, not a roller, so that takes a good bit more time."

"Yes, I suppose." Mrs. Stoneworth pulled a stretchy thing from her ponytail and redid it. "Well, then, you may have to start working nights, to finish up."

"Nights?"

"We could rig up lights. Spotlights from cars, if necessary. Anything it takes. I don't care about the expense," she said, walking away.

"Or run-down car batteries," Bud muttered. "Jon, now I don't want you to go believin' that all the folks in this town are bats in the belfry. Some are, but not all." He started up the ladder. "Whyn't you come along," he said over his shoulder, "and visit with me while I'm laying callouses on my hands from this brush."

"Okay." I followed him up. It was a high house, and the ladder was very tall. But I thought, *You crawl up and down a ladder just as long as this one almost every night.* Yes, but I couldn't see how long it was, in the dark.

"Bud," I said, trying to keep my voice down, "do you think she meant it, about working at night?"

"Sure she did. That woman is hell-bent to win the award."

"What's the prize? A trip to the Painted Desert?"

"The prize, so far's I know it, is to get the house on the cover of a state beautification magazine."

I heard the back door slam again.

"Bud, I'm going down," I said. "I think we're under surveillance."

"Come back around lunchtime," he said.

"I'll try."

◆

Back home, Teresa and Mom were talking in the upstairs hall. As I went past them toward my room, Teresa said, "Jon, you tell her."

"Tell her what?"

"That she and Dad should go out after my birthday dinner. They've been invited to a big get-together. I don't care if the invitation came late—they should still go."

"Why don't you?" I said to Mom. "It's not like we're going to play pin the tail on the donkey after dinner."

"There's plenty of time to build a social life, but

Tess will only be home for a little while now," Mom said, starting down the stairs.

"Like weeks," Teresa called after her. She turned and rolled her eyes at me. "Can you believe they turned down an invitation to a really great event just to stay home all evening with me?"

"Maybe you're an out for the folks. Maybe they really didn't want to go."

"Oh, right." Teresa went into my room and flopped on her stomach across my bed. "They need to get out and meet people. This town has a very closed society, I hear, and it's hard to break into if you're from somewhere else."

"They'll be all right." I suddenly remembered that white cat hairs could still be on the bedspread. "Would you please remove your inert mass from my bed?" I said. "I don't want the box springs sprung."

"Idiot," my sister said in a mild kind of way as she pushed herself up. "I'm going to miss you when I go away to school. But not very much."

"Same here," I said in my usual friendly manner.

After she left I wondered if I should have let her pour out her heart about Ace. Naw. She'd get over it. Both of my sisters had great bouncing-back abilities.

I decided to rest a little, then make a sandwich and go over and eat it with Bud. I was beginning to like him a lot. There were things I wanted to ask him about school here, and the guys, and what usually went on. Bud was probably like Eddie . . . knew lots of kids. Was popular.

I thought of Eddie again and the dull letter I had written him. Then I let myself imagine how it would be if I laid it on Eddie . . . the whole story of my midnight ramblings with a young druid. It was a pretty embarrassing thing to imagine . . . the unbelieving look . . . the howls of laughter . . . and then, "Tell me you're just putting me on. *Druids!*"

I thought of how I'd answer him. I'd say, "You know, Eddie, you lead a pretty restricted life. Sports, hanging out, that's where it is for you. I want to tell you, man, there's a world out there with amazing things going on. But you'll never know about them if you go around with a closed mind."

But why was I even thinking about what he'd say and what I'd say? Why waste brain power when I knew absolutely I'd never tell Eddie about meeting Flora at night in the meadow or about building our Stonehenge or anything else?

Was there anyone I *could* tell? No. Not a single soul. It was a secret I could never share. Or rather, that I would never want to share.

It was just for me.

SEVENTEEN

♦ ♦ ♦

*T*hat night I decided to be adventurous and leave my room by way of the tree. The roof was flat, so no problem there. I scooted to the edge and looked down into the darkness of the branches where the moonlight didn't penetrate.

Just do it! I told myself, and took hold of a branch and was about to move out when—what was that, to my left?

Holy Toledo! Mrs. Stoneworth actually had Bud painting at night, high on a ladder! The way the spotlight hit him you'd think he was a high-wire act in a circus.

It struck me funny at first. I'd actually made a megaphone of my hands to call out something weird to him when I realized that wasn't a good idea. Bud had better not see me adventuring out at night, for obvious reasons.

I scrambled down the tree and crouched like a cat burglar as I made my way to the meadow. I did this out of instinct, or maybe from watching too many TV crime shows. Bud couldn't scope me from where he was painting because there was a tree between us. Besides, you can't see beyond a bright light when it's beamed right on you.

At last I'd gone far enough that the light on the house was out of sight. As I came to the clearing, Flora called, "Be careful, don't come too close. I'm not sure the cement's set."

I went over, watching my step. Flora had managed to make what looked like a perfect circle. I guessed she'd used string and a stick. "How did you wet it down?"

"With a pail of water and a tin can, to dip. Does it look all right to you?" Before I could answer, she went on, "I had to cut the grass before I put down the cement."

That really got my attention. "Flora, someone could have heard you!"

"Who? No one ever comes to this meadow."

"But the sound of a mower in the middle of the night . . . Come on."

"Come on, yourself! I'm not stupid enough to use a mower. I cut the grass with clippers, and I want to inform you it was hard work. The clippers were rusty."

"Oh." Still, an uneasiness had come over me. "You don't actually *know* that no one walks through the meadow. I mean, you don't have a watchman on the lookout, do you?"

"What is it, Jon? Do you want to back out? Is that it? Because if—"

"No! I'm just a little concerned is all. If someone did happen to stroll by and notice the gravestones we'd be in deep . . . trouble."

"No one will," Flora said. "Believe me. And now we'd better get to work, digging trenches for the stones."

"All of them?" I asked, taken aback.

"Well, of course all. Otherwise, what's the point?"

"Tell me where to dig." I said, acting manly as I took hold of the spade.

I dug into the grassy earth. I had to jab the spade and shove it down with my foot and then lift up the sod. It wasn't easy. When I thought I was finished we found the trench wasn't deep enough. The stone toppled. I dug farther. We put in the first stone and pushed dirt around it to make it stay.

"See?" Flora said. "One done already. I'll do the next."

I'd like to say I wrenched the spade from her frail little hands, but I needed the rest.

Flora didn't make great progress because she didn't have the weight to bear down on the spade. I wanted to suggest we give it up, but with her that wouldn't be possible. Reluctantly, I got up and put my feet on either side of the spade handle and jiggled until the spade bit the soil. After I got the turf up, Flora could dig out the rest of the dirt.

We went on this way for six, seven stones. I could

feel blisters forming on my palms. Why hadn't I brought along work gloves?

The moonlight was getting dim as the moon and earth moved. Still we worked on. My back was beginning to feel like a thick piece of cardboard, cracked in the middle.

Suddenly Flora said, "Look who's walking our way."

"*What?* I . . . I thought you said no one ever came in here!" With alarm, I watched the shadowy figure of a woman approaching.

Flora frowned. "Well, Jon, I certainly didn't mean my aunt!"

"Your aunt?"

"My aunt Evangeline, the druid priestess."

"Why is *she* coming here?"

"I imagine she's come to help prepare for the ceremony. With her knowledge of all the rituals, it's bound to be a most moving experience."

I wasn't so sure about that. The moving experience I wanted at the moment was to get my body out of there. It was becoming clearer that what we were doing was more than just a lark.

The woman (what had they called her . . . *daft?*) got closer and I found myself backing up a few steps.

"Jon . . ." Flora took hold of my blistered hand and brought me forward. "This is my aunt Evangeline, the high priestess."

"Hi, priestess," I said. It just came out. I wasn't trying to be funny.

"You may call me Evangeline," the woman said. "Now, let's see. What have you done so far?"

As Flora took the woman around to inspect the stones, I checked out her looks. Her hair was darker than her sister's but was pulled up into a similar kind of bun. I couldn't tell too much about her features in the dim light, but at least she didn't *look* deranged if she actually was. Her dress came almost down to her ankles and below it I could spot gym shoes . . . not Nikes or anything cool, but the kind kids used to wear.

The two of them came back to where I was standing. "It all seems in order," the aunt said. "Now have you selected the spot for the altar and Slaughter Stone?"

I hated those words. Especially *slaughter*.

"By the calculations you gave me," Flora said, "they should be right over there." She pointed.

"Excellent. Now we had better get on with the placing of the stones."

Oh, wonderful. My palms were really burning. I wondered if the blisters were about to burst and get infected. And my back still ached. But to my surprise, Flora's aunt picked up the spade and began digging. To my even greater surprise, she did it without a great show of effort. Maybe growing those herbs of hers built up muscle.

We fell into a pattern of the aunt digging and Flora and I fitting in the stones and stomping the dirt to hold them in place.

A gray darkness was around us by the time all the headstones were positioned. Suddenly I felt something brush against my ankles. Kat.

I picked him up and he rubbed his head against my chin. Kat really liked me, that was for sure. I felt closer to him than I ever had to Fritz, the dog we used to have. I always suspected that old Fritz hung around me because I fed him. Kat had no special reason to seek me out, but he did.

When I looked back at Flora she was standing there alone.

"What happened to your aunt?" I asked. "Did she dematerialize or what?"

"She had to get home. We should, too. It's very late."

Reluctantly, I put Kat down. I really wanted to take him with me, but of course I couldn't.

"Same time tomorrow night?" Flora asked. "We must set up the altar and practice our dances. We shouldn't linger too long, though. We must store up strength for the night to follow, the night of the summer solstice."

I felt a little tingle up my spine. Why? Because the stage was almost set for the ceremony Flora had talked about but which deep inside I thought would never happen. The circle was real, the stones were real, and the aunt, druid or not, certainly seemed to know what she was doing.

"What about my costume?" I asked, like some actor about to do a play.

"It will be taken care of," Flora said. "And now, farewell."

"Yeah, farewell."

I went through the meadow and around the side of my house to the basement door. I pushed. It didn't budge. What? I pushed harder, and put my shoulder to it. The thing was locked. Who had done that? Then with alarm I remembered that I'd locked it myself the last time I came back from the meadow. And tonight I'd gone down the tree and forgotten the door was still locked.

I looked across the street, thinking, I guess, that I could borrow a ladder. I don't know how I'd have explained that. But of course the house was dark, with Bud long gone, and the ladder had been put away.

Climb the tree? With blistered hands? Not a good idea.

I walked around to the front porch, hoping the door was unlocked. Nope. But there was a faint light coming from the living room window.

Looking in, I saw the TV flickering pathetically, having finished all programming for the night. And in an armchair Teresa was sprawled, asleep and dreaming no doubt of her unfaithful louse of a love.

Would her shrieks awaken the household if I tapped on the window? They might, but what other choice did I have?

As she heard the rapping, Teresa jerked up, startled but silent.

"Teresa," I called out. "It's me . . . Jon."

Thank goodness my sister never watched slice-and-dice movies so she had none of those instant replays as she snapped awake. She turned to see my face in the window.

"Let me in," I called.

I have to hand it to Tess. She got up and walked to the front door and didn't even seem particularly surprised to see me.

"Up kind of late, aren't you?" I said, taking the initiative.

"Yeah. I can't sleep, thinking about Ace."

"It was such a nice night I went out for a walk in the meadow." Uh-oh. I shouldn't have said *meadow*. "And the door clicked shut, I guess."

"So that's it." Teresa went back into the living room to turn off the TV and then we climbed the stairs together. She was too groggy, I guess, to notice my sweaty smell and dirty hands.

When we got to the top I whispered, "Don't tell the folks about my walk. They'd worry."

"Yeah, they would." She stumbled off to her room and I went to mine. I just had to hope my sister would keep quiet the next day when she was awake enough to wonder why I'd done such a stupid thing.

At least I hadn't locked my bedroom door from the inside before I left. *Good thinking, Jon,* I said to myself.

I put on my nighttime T-shirt and shorts before going to the bathroom. There in the light I examined my hands, which looked like bad news. Some of the blisters were split open and embedded with dirt. I cleaned them as best I could and then poured on disinfectant which nearly sent me through the ceiling.

When I finally settled down in bed I couldn't help thinking how strange it all was. Here I was involved in a nightly adventure that no one in the family even guessed was happening. As far as they knew, my only occupation was hanging around the house, trying to get totally well.

I couldn't help feeling a little bit self-satisfied. So far, I hadn't given one bleep about knowing the so-called missing girl, or let slip a single word about Kat. I'd hidden my aches and pains and covered my nightly tracks. Somehow I'd get past these blistered hands, too.

Only two more days to get through. *The silent preparations continue! The mysteries of the ceremony are about to be revealed!*

And then what? When the summer solstice was history, what would I be to Flora? And what would she be to me?

I looked toward the window where the curtains were blowing in a slight breeze. Would Kat ever come to visit me again?

EIGHTEEN

♦ ♦ ♦

*B*y the time I got up the next day Teresa and Dad had gone to work and Colleen was nowhere around. I found Mother in the backyard pulling at some weeds around what looked like a neglected rosebush.

Would she ask me to help? Just thinking of garden work made my palms sting. The torn blisters were stiff today and could probably have used some salve.

"Isn't it awfully hot to be working out here?" I asked.

"Yes, it is. But I thought if I did it gradually . . ."

"You should hire a gardener." *As long as your son isn't offering to help.*

"Oh, Jon, there isn't that much to do. And I'd rather like to get into gardening. I never seemed to have the time back home, but here . . ."

"Your social life will pick up," I said.

Mom laughed. "Are you saying that back home I used to be a social butterfly?"

"I didn't mean that."

"Actually, I've been asked to join a garden club. I

might just do it." She got up and peeled off gloves she'd been smart enough to put on. "That's enough for today. Have you had breakfast . . . lunch? You slept late."

"I was beat."

"Oh, honey," Mom said, taking my arm as we walked back inside, "I'm afraid you've been up and around too much lately."

"You're probably right," I said in answer to the understatement of the year. Of course, Mom had no way of knowing that.

I went across the street to kill time with Bud. He was up on the ladder again.

"How's it going?" I called.

"Not too bad. I just have to do these windows along the side and the ones on the front."

Mrs. Stoneworth, who must have had the instincts of a hound dog, suddenly appeared from the back of the house. "Oh, Jon," she said. "How nice to see you. I was just going over to talk to your mother. I hear your folks are going to a party tomorrow night with some very important people."

This was news to me. "I don't think so," I said. "We're having a birthday celebration for my sister."

"I'm talking about later. This other event begins around nine o'clock. I hear a judge or two will be there, and I'm hoping your folks will put in a good word for me."

"Judges?" I was really confused. "Like in court?"

Mrs. Stoneworth giggled. "No, darlin'. Judges for

the Painted Lady contest. My husband and I were not invited to the party. I guess we fall somethin' short of being in the right social circle. But at least your parents will be there."

"Oh. Well, I'm sure they'll do all they can."

Beaming, Mrs. Stoneworth started across the street to our house.

Fortunately for me and my sore hands, I didn't have to go up the ladder to talk to Bud. He was coming down.

"Isn't that woman the limit?" he said. "Seems like she'll do most anything to win that contest."

"I noticed you painting last night," I said. "With lights."

"Oh, that was something. I like to have died, being up there so high and not another soul around. Wish you'd come over to keep me company."

"Will you be painting tonight?" *Say no,* I thought.

"No, not tonight. My daddy and some others are going to a baseball game over in Jefferson and I'm going along. I don't care how Mrs. Stoneworth fusses about it, I'm not working tonight."

Good, I thought. *I won't have to dig up a reason why I can't come over and keep Bud company.*

♦

Around ten o'clock, on the night before the ceremony, I wrapped some gauze around my hands and then pulled work gloves over them. They still hurt a little, going down the ladder, but I didn't feel safe going down the stairs with my parents in the living room watching a movie on the VCR. I knew they wouldn't check on me when they came upstairs, because of scenes I'd thrown in the past . . . *Cut it out! I'm not a kid! I'm not an invalid!*

In the basement I made sure the outside door was left ajar so I'd have no trouble getting back in this time.

As usual, Flora was already in the meadow. For a few minutes I stood back in the shadows and watched her dance around the circle. I reminded myself to bring the camera tomorrow night. Photos wouldn't be as good as an actual video of the ceremony, but at least I could hide the pictures and look at them in private.

"Well, Jon," Flora said as she stopped dancing. "Are you ready to begin?"

"Sure. Begin what?"

"The practice ceremony. First, the three of us— you, Auntie, and I—will do the ceremonial dance. Then we will go to different oak trees and perform the chant."

"What chant is that?"

"Auntie knows it. She'll say it and we'll echo the last words. It's a very moving experience . . . our avowal of devotion to the sacred trees."

"I see. And then?"

"And then we place the wreaths from our heads—"

"I'm wearing a wreath?"

"Well, of course you are. We will all wear wreaths. Even Kat. He has become quite accustomed to it by now."

I remembered the first time Kat had visited me in my room, and the scent of flowers. I still had that flower, dried now, in the drawer of my bedside table.

"Where will we get the wreaths? From a florist?"

"Of course not, Jon. Aunt Evangeline is creating them. Kat's will be made of flowers, as always, and the rest of ours will be made from leaves and special herbs, the kind my aunt grows."

"Yeah, someone told me she grows herbs and sells them to a health store in town."

"Exactly. The health store people have open minds. Not like most of the others around here. Did you also hear that my aunt is slightly demented?"

"Uh, no. I didn't hear that." I lied.

"Well, she's not. It's a false impression that people have about my aunt. She's been to many places and had many mystic experiences. But she's given up trying to explain them to people."

"Well, I'm open-minded," I said.

"I could tell that from the first," Flora said. "When I saw that Kat trusted you I knew I could, too." She walked to the circle and I followed. "As you see, I have created an altar. That is where we will offer up the sacrifice of our wreaths, amid burning incense."

"I see."

"Then we will dance around the circle in our robes. Oh, you might like to try yours on." Flora walked away and picked up a bundle that had been lying on the grass. "Here it is."

I unrolled the dark-colored robe, which looked like a kimono, and put it on. It smelled musty. "Where'd you get this?" I asked Flora as I tied the long fabric belt.

"My aunt unearthed it from a trunk. At first she was a bit reluctant to include you in the ceremony, but I assured her you were absolutely trustworthy."

I wondered if Flora ever talked like an ordinary kid. If she used this kind of language at school, it was no wonder her classmates gave her a wide berth.

"What about afterward?" I asked. "After the ceremony's over?"

What I meant was, would we still be friends? But Flora took a different meaning. "Afterward, we will have to return the stones to the cemetery."

I could feel all my muscles protesting. "Right away?"

"Not tomorrow night. That would be too abrupt. We want the essence of the night to linger awhile."

"Oh, okay." I was relieved, but then a feeling of uneasiness crept over me. Even though Flora had said no one ever walked through the meadow, there was always a chance that someone *might*. A kid, maybe, taking a shortcut. What would a kid do if he suddenly came upon a circle of tombstones around a cement circle? He'd blab, that's what he'd do.

"You're very quiet, suddenly," Flora said. "Is something bothering you, Jon?"

"Oh, no!" I protested. "I was just letting the essence start to sink in . . . getting in the mood for tomorrow night."

"I promise you," Flora said, "it'll be a night you will always remember." I had no doubt about that, no doubt at all.

♦ ♦ ♦

NINETEEN

I was dreaming Kat was stranded on a high cliff and I was trying to climb it, trying to rescue him. My hands hurt from clutching bare rock and sliding, sliding . . .

"Jon, darling, wake up."

Mother was in the room. "You were groaning."

"Stupid dream. What time is it?"

"Nearly ten. You seemed so exhausted I hated to wake you. Here, take your temperature."

I started to push the thermometer away, but I remembered how raw and red my blistered palms looked. I opened my mouth like a bird and kept my hands flat on the bed.

"You look flushed."

"M-o-m . . ." I protested around the thermometer.

"Haven't you been taking your pills?"

"Ummm." Why do people stick thermometers in your mouth and then ask questions? It's as bad as dentists. Watching Mom going around, straightening up things, I was glad I'd hidden the robe far back in the closet.

Mom took out the thermometer and held it up. "Oh, Jon, it's a hundred and two. How do you feel? Do you ache anywhere?"

My back felt like a load of gravel. My neck had metal rods in it that wouldn't bend. My legs yelped with every little move. "I feel great," I said.

Mother looked dubious. "You're going to rest in bed today anyway. And if the temp is this high tomorrow, we're calling the doctor." She smoothed my hair. I tolerated it. "You've probably been straining yourself," she said. "Doing too much."

Mother, I thought, *you've no idea.* "Does this mean I get breakfast in bed?" I asked.

She smiled. "I'll bring it up."

"No! Let Colleen. Or Teresa."

"Colleen's across the street with Eric and Teresa's at work."

"Then I'll get up. I don't want you to do it." I leaped out of bed and nearly collapsed as my knees buckled underneath me.

"To bed," Mom said, pointing. "And stay there until the celebration begins tonight."

I stared at her, open-mouthed. What did she know?

"Jon, what's wrong? Don't tell me you've forgotten about Teresa's party!"

"Oh . . . oh . . . no. I didn't forget. I guess I . . . uh . . . thought you'd postpone it. Aren't you and Dad going to some high-class happening?" Lucky that I remembered!

Mother sighed. "I guess we'll have to go. Your father's boss wants him to be there and meet people. That seems to be very important in a small town . . . to get in with the right crowd." She made a little face. "Does that sound phony to you?"

"Hey, Mom, you gotta do what you gotta do."

I ate breakfast. And then Colleen woke me up with lunch on a tray. Could I have fallen asleep again?

"Lunch already? What time is it?" I asked.

"Daytime," my sister said, and giggled. "That's what Eric says. He's always saying funny things."

Clearly, Colleen needed more mature playmates before she regressed to crawling and drooling.

After lunch I got up, showered, and put on clean clothes. I decided to call Eddie to tell him the lovely Teresa was now another year older than him. He wasn't home. His mom said he was off on a fishing trip and would probably send me a postcard. Then, after locking my door against any impromptu visits from Colleen and her witty friend, I took another nap. Unbelievable!

When I got up again most of the muscle aches were gone. My palms looked better, too, rosy now instead of red. I went downstairs and it was like the past had reappeared. There were balloons all over the place and pink crepe-paper streamers across the dining room.

"What do you think?" Mom asked, coming out of the kitchen.

"Isn't it a little preteen?"

Mom flushed. "I guess you're right. I just wanted to . . . I don't know . . . make a little fuss one last time, before Teresa goes off to the university. After that everything will be different."

"What do you mean?"

"Oh . . . once she's gone away her mind will be split between her being-away place and home."

I wanted to say that Teresa's mind had been split already between here and back home with Ace. Only now her heart was split . . . split wide open because of that slime.

Mom went back to the kitchen and I was glad she did because Teresa walked in just then. When she saw the pink streamers, the balloons, and the frilly little nut cups on the table, an I-don't-believe-this expression came over her face.

She turned her gaze on me. I shrugged. Then I nodded toward the kitchen. Teresa got it.

"Wow!" she said. "You've decorated the room!" She went out to Mom and when I glanced toward the kitchen I saw she was hugging Mom and acting appreciative. Teresa's all right. I realized I'd miss her this fall.

She kept up her high-spirited performance all during dinner and even through the cake ceremony and gift unwrapping. She seemed to like the earrings I got her. "These may be the closest I'll get to dolphins," she said, putting them on. "For a while."

"Eric went to Hawaii," Colleen said. "But he didn't

swim with the dolphins. He never goes into water that has fish in it."

Dad caught the high points of the evening on video. I got my camera and took a few shots, making sure there were plenty left for the druid ceremony.

The folks stalled as long as they could, but they had to get ready for the command-performance party. Teresa and I cleared the table and shoved the dishes into the washer. I wondered if my sister would expect me to hang around her all evening, but she said she planned to call all her best friends later. It was another of her birthday gifts.

I watched TV for a while with Colleen to try to get her sleepy. She seemed to be experiencing a sugar high, though, from all the cake and candy. After a while she went upstairs and I began to prepare mentally for my late-night event. I remembered the camera and went to the dining room to get it. It wasn't there. After looking all over I gave up and went upstairs. Colleen's room was dark, and that was suspicious. She couldn't have conked out so suddenly. I looked in and saw her at her window.

"Colleen, what are you doing?"

"Taking pictures of that painter in front of Eric's house, on the ladder."

I looked out, and sure enough . . . there was Bud high in the sky, bathed in lights. I wanted to go over and talk but it would mean too much of a delay.

"You can't take pictures this far away at night," I said, snatching the camera away from my sister.

"I can, too! I just did!"

I looked at the number of exposures left and saw there were only four. "Damn!" I said. "You're such a brat, Colleen!"

"I'm telling! I'm telling what you said!" She started after me but I took off for my room and locked the door behind me. After a while she got tired of banging on it and went away.

I looked out my farther window. The moon was full and the night was bright. No clouds anywhere. What time was the ceremony supposed to start? Flora hadn't actually mentioned a time. I glanced at my watch. It was getting close to ten.

My heart started racing and my breathing quickened. Did actors feel this way just before they went onstage? But they'd rehearsed. I wasn't sure about tonight's script. Oh, well. I'd better get going.

I rolled up the robe, tied it with the belt, and slipped the belt over my wrist. Then I stuck the camera in one hip pocket and the flashlight in the other. With the folks gone and Teresa in her room it would have been so simple to go down the regular stairs, but I couldn't chance it. Colleen might be staring out the front window.

I put on the work gloves, and went down through the hidden passage and out the basement door. Bud wasn't on the ladder now. Maybe he'd gone to get more paint. Still, I hugged the shadows and then raced off through the meadow.

My timing was great. Just as I reached the clearing

I saw two figures coming toward me . . . Flora and her aunt. With them was Kat, walking proudly like a tamed white tiger.

Our improvised Stonehenge looked impressive in the full light of the moon. Seeing it there, waiting, gave me a little chill.

As I waited for the others to join me, I couldn't help thinking how strange it was, that I was doing this. And stranger still, how important to my life Flora and Kat and this night had become.

TWENTY

♦ ♦ ♦

*F*lora, as she came near, looked more luminous than ever. Her gown, a gauzy green, moved softly in the slight breeze. The moonlight seemed to pick up each strand of her hair and give it a light of its own as it flowed out from her crown of leaves.

Her aunt was wearing a long dark robe and also a wreath of leaves. "Put on your robe, sir," she said to me. "So we can begin the ceremony."

I did, and Flora handed me my wreath. Kat was already wearing his circlet of flowers. Then the aunt, holding aloft an incense burner, walked around on the cement ring, with Flora and me following. By the time we'd done it three times I could feel the cement cracking and crumbling beneath my feet. Flora must have made it very thin, and of course cement on grass doesn't hold all that well.

After we finished circling, the high priestess went to the altar, lit the incense, and then chanted some strange words. It could have been a poem she'd learned in Nepal. After that she switched to English.

"We light the fire for Mother Earth, for Father Sun, for Daughter Moon on this significant night of the summer solstice," she said. Then she waved her hands through the smoke and touched her forehead. She motioned to Flora and me to do the same.

"Now comes the ceremony of the oaks," the druid leader said. "Each of us will embrace a tree and recite the words of oneness."

Under normal circumstances I would have felt pretty feeble, hugging a tree, but these were not normal circumstances. This whole ceremony, bogus though it might be, got me into a state of mind where I was ready to believe almost anything.

When we came back to the altar, the high priestess said, "It is now time to make the sacrifice. Kat?"

My heart lurched, but only for a moment.

"Kat, let me take your wreath," Flora said. "We must offer it up to the spirits of our druid ancestors."

After the flowers were placed on the altar, our leader took the wreath from her head. "This wreath I present to you, O druids gone beyond," the woman intoned. She laid it down on the altar and motioned for Flora to do the same. As she was about to step up I heard a faint call from across the meadow.

The others heard it, too, and we saw a figure running toward us from the direction of Flora's house. Without thinking, I pulled the wreath off my head and whirled it into the bushes beyond.

Flora, making little moans of fear, grasped her aunt's arm and hung back, even when it was clear it was her mother running toward us. The aunt, shaking free, went forward and called out, "What is it, Belinda?"

"It's him, it's him . . ." the mother gasped, out of breath.

We were all standing together now.

"My father?" Flora asked hoarsely. "He's here?"

"Not here. On his way. He's coming to get you."

"Oh no!" It was the first time I'd ever seen Flora lose control. "How do you *know?*"

"That Elsie woman . . . the one who helped you get away before . . . ? She called . . . had trouble getting our new phone number from information . . . anyway, she said he's driving down and could get here at any time. So baby, we've got to leave!"

"I can't!" Flora said wildly. "I can't go and leave all this!"

"Go!" the aunt said to her sister. "Take the truck. I'll stay behind and tend to matters here."

"But Auntie!" Flora wailed.

"You've got no choice, child. Go now, while you can."

"Oh Jon!" Flora ran to me and flung her arms around my waist. "You are my truest friend ever!"

"Same here," I said, feeling at such a loss.

"And I will . . ." Her mother was pulling her away and they began running. "I will . . ." Flora called over her shoulder, "remember you forever!" With her free hand she held the wreath on her head as she and her mother raced away, across the meadow. Kat streaked along behind them.

Before they were even out of sight the aunt had stripped off her gown. She was wearing baggy pants and a shirt underneath. "Give me your robe, too," she said in a regular voice. "I'll ditch them back home when I run to get the wagon. Start pulling up those stones and get them stacked. I don't know how much time we'll have."

I stood there dumbly staring. Two minutes ago we'd been chanting . . . and now . . .

"Is there a problem?" she asked.

"No, no." I pulled off the robe and handed it to her and she took off, leaving me all alone in the meadow.

Alone, I now thought, with all the evidence. I could see how urgent it was to get those gravestones back to the cemetery. In no time at all the father could arrive in town, and get the sheriff and possibly a search party fanning through the meadow looking for Flora. If they saw the circle of stones and the altar they'd figure out eventually who'd set it up. They'd call it a pagan rite, probably, and say Flora was in the hands of wackos.

I shoved my hands into the work gloves and began wrenching the stones from the ground. They were all ready to go when Auntie came back with the wagon. We loaded on as many as we could and set off for the cemetery.

Once we'd cleared the ditch and the barbed-wire

fence, there was the long trek to the far end of the cemetery.

Suddenly, as we made our bumpy way, the woman said, "I had the feeling all along that I shouldn't have started the druid game . . . I should have known it could get out of hand."

"Game?" I almost dropped the handle of the wagon. "Did you say *game?*"

"Well, of course," the aunt said, sounding a bit like Flora. "Surely *you*," meaning a guy my age, "didn't take it seriously?"

"Well . . . uh . . . Flora seemed to believe . . ."

"Flora imagines well."

"You mean none of this was the real thing, even to her?" I stumbled over a clump of dirt. "It's hard for me to believe she was play-acting all the time."

"The child throws herself into imaginative adventure. It helps her survive her dreadful life."

This was all such a surprise. "Then what about you? Are you saying you're not a druid?"

The woman gave a half-laugh. "I've been called a lot of things, and some may even be true. But no, I'm not a druid and never was."

I felt as though I'd been insulated in a little world of magic and enchantment that had suddenly been torn apart. And now I'd been thrust back to cold reality.

It was a weird kind of reality. There I was, dragging through a cemetery late at night, hauling gravestones over bumpy terrain with an eccentric woman I didn't even know.

To make it worse, my legs, especially the joints, started screaming, *I hurt! I hurt!* My back joined in. I guess I actually groaned because Flora's aunt said, "We're almost there, boy."

We took the weedy path into the deserted part and stopped.

"Now, which stone goes where?" the woman asked

"What?"

"You kept a record when you took them, didn't you? Surely you must have."

"Uh . . . no. No, we didn't."

"Oh for heaven's sake. Well, let's place them here and there for the moment. We'll have to come back and try to sort them out later."

We put a stone wherever a sunken place seemed to indicate there was a grave.

I was wrung out, but we still had another load of stones to return. As we rumbled back through the cemetery I wished I was young and little, so little I could be pulled in the wagon.

Flora's aunt talked above the creak of the wheels.

"Poor little Flora," she said. "I wish we could have had the whole ceremony, so she'd have something very special to remember."

"Yeah," I said. "That would have been nice."

"It's sad," the aunt said, "but sometimes people have to live in their minds because they've no other place to go."

At the time I was too concerned with how much my body was aching to think about what she was saying. Later on, though, when I remembered, it seemed to me that Flora's aunt was no more nutty than people who produce plays or any other kind of make-believe. And she was doing it for love, not money.

"I really felt sorry for Flora, hiding out all the time," I said. "It was like she was a captive, except at night."

"That's why it was so important to let her mind reach out to other places."

"Right." I didn't think that would be enough for me, though . . . just to let my mind wander around.

We finally got back to the meadow, where the rest of the stones were lying. I was panting by the time we'd heaved them onto the wagon. I had to stop, to breathe.

"Is something wrong?" The aunt probably didn't know I was barely out of sick bay.

"No," I gasped. "Let's go."

The second trip to the cemetery was pure torture. Every muscle in my body shook as I helped push the wagon through the ditch again, and through the fence. The women of Flora's family seemed to have some kind of super strength. She'd never shown any sign of fatigue and now her aunt wasn't even breathing hard. True, neither of them was recovering from rheumatic fever, but still . . .

We had reached the neglected part of the cemetery once more and were just removing the stones from the wagon when we both went on red alert. What we heard was police sirens in the distance. And they were coming closer. Then we caught a faint flashing light as the cars turned into the cemetery's far-off entrance gate.

I felt absolutely stiff. Sweat was pouring down my back and along my sides. I was sure my own doomsday had arrived.

"Run, boy!" Aunt Evangeline hissed. "Get yourself back home!"

"Wh . . . what about you?"

"I'll light out for the meadow with the wagon and hide out if I can."

"But . . . but what if they find you?"

"Ha! I'll just go into my weird act. You'd be surprised what you can get by with when people think you're a little bit off." She shoved me in the back. "Go!"

I knew that I had to get moving. The sirens were coming closer. I forced my throbbing legs into a run and kept ahead of the aunt for a while. When I slowed I could hear the rattle of the wagon right behind me. My chest felt ready to burst.

At the fence, I simply collapsed. Flora's aunt leaned over me. "Are you all right?"

"I don't . . . think so . . ."

The rest is very vague. I remember a ripping sound and a burning sensation as I wriggled through the barbed-wire fence. I remember crawling up the ditch on all fours. I know Flora's aunt supported me until I reached our house. Then, on our front porch, I passed out completely.

TWENTY-ONE

♦ ♦ ♦

*I*t seemed like the next moment, but I found out later it was the next day. I heard voices. I felt submerged. Finally I managed to open my eyes.

"He's awake," a strange voice said.

"Darling . . ." My mother's face floated and then came into rather blurry focus.

My first words were the classic, "Where am I?"

"In the hospital, son," my father said. "You're going to be all right."

I realized I was wearing an oxygen mask. I probably looked like a geek. "What's comin' off?" I managed to say.

"How do you feel?" Now it was the doctor who hove into view. He removed the oxygen mask. "Aches?"

"Just everywhere. How did I get here?"

"By ambulance," Dad said. "It was a lucky thing the Atkins boy saw you and came running over. Teresa called the ambulance and then us."

Bud . . . Bud had come to my rescue.

The doctor asked my parents to step outside then, while he examined me. "You've been exerting yourself lately?" he asked.

"I've taken a few walks." *Hauled tombstones around, climbed through barbed-wire fences, clambered up and down ditches.*

"Walks, eh?" This doctor really didn't know me, so he couldn't tell how far I was stretching the truth. Still, he was no fool. "You've got to realize," he said, "that rheumatic fever is something to take very seriously. You have to give it time. And rest. If you do that, there's no reason why you can't go on with a normal life."

"Like when?"

With a little smile, the doctor said, "If you stop doing whatever you've been doing and rest, you should be fine by the time school starts this fall. It's up to you."

"Yeah, okay." I'd stop doing what I'd been doing because it was over. Over forever, I thought.

The doctor went out to the hall and I could hear him talking to my parents. Weariness once again took hold of me. I shut down.

When I woke up again it was late afternoon. Teresa was in the room.

"Hey scuzzbrain, how are you doing?" she asked, coming to the side of the bed.

"Okay. Where're the folks?"

"They'll be back later. They were here all last night and didn't leave until about noon, when it finally looked as though you weren't going to check out for good."

"I wouldn't die and leave you with no one to hassle."

"I know. It's appreciated. So what's the story?"

"Story?" I tried to look bewildered. "There's no story. I just went out for a walk."

"You did, huh? Leaving your bedroom door locked from the inside?"

My heart gave a thump. "I can explain all that. But not just now. I'm too weak." *I need time to come up with an explanation.*

"The sheriff talked to your friend Bud."

"What?"

"Yeah, he wondered if he'd seen anything going on around the neighborhood from his perch up on that ladder."

"And?" Could my sister hear my heart thumping? "What did Bud say?"

"Ask him yourself. He said he was coming over to see you." Teresa opened up her huge saddlebag purse and pulled out a newspaper clipping. "You've been awfully mysterious lately, roaming around late at night. I wonder if you happen to know about any of this." She handed me the news item from the local paper. The story read:

Police responding to a report last night of flickering lights in Rosebank Cemetery were mystified by signs of apparent vandalism.

Tombstones in an obscure section, dating back more than a century, had been uprooted and rearranged, though not damaged.

A police officer whose ancestor is buried in the section noted that the wrong grave marker was at the site. It is believed that at least ten other tombstones have been switched.

Cemetery officials were at a loss to explain the purpose of the exchange. "It must have been the work of pranksters," they said. "But what was the point?"

Old records will be consulted to reset the markers in their rightful positions.

"So?" I said to Teresa.

"So?" she said back, with her wicked smile. "You haven't a clue, huh? How come your hands are blistered?"

I shoved them under the sheets.

"And how about the dirt and clay all over your shoes? How come your shirt was ripped? You must have taken quite a walk."

"I'm not talking without my attorney," I muttered. The door opened on cue and in came . . . Bud.

"Hey, you're alive!" he said.

"Yeah." I turned to my sister. "Bye, Teresa. Nice of you to stop by."

"Oh, I'm in no hurry." She turned to Bud. "I'm this geek's sister, much as I hate to admit it. And I guess you're the fellow conspirator . . . Bud?"

"He had nothing to do with it," I said.

"Oh!" She looked triumphant. "Then you *did!*"

I shifted around on the bed. "I guess I might as well tell you." I glared at Teresa. "But if you give so much as one little laugh . . . !"

"Me? Your adoring sister? Come on, Jon. Talk."

So, with nothing now left to lose, I told the two of them the whole story, beginning with the night Kat first walked into my room. If I hadn't felt so miserable I'd have enjoyed the way their eyes widened and their jaws dropped. "So now Flora's gone, I guess." I turned to Bud. "Do you know if she got away?"

"Yeah, she did. She and her mama. Her daddy came looking for her all right, but there wasn't a trace."

"Didn't they question the aunt?" Teresa asked.

"I guess they did, but Miss Evangeline wouldn't tell 'em anything. What's your opinion of her anyway, Jon? Is she crazy or not?"

"Not. Eccentric, maybe, but that's her right. She was smart enough to keep her niece from going mental."

Bud came closer to the bed. "Jon, you don't have to worry about the evidence in the meadow. I cleared it away."

"Wh . . . what?"

"That cement ring. I finished breaking it up and put the pieces in an old gunny sack and hid it. There's nothing left in the meadow but holes in the ground and some flattened grass. I heard someone say this morning that a UFO must've landed there and left that ring in the grass."

"Honestly . . ." Teresa said. "Why am I not surprised?"

"How did you connect me with the meadow, Bud?" This kid really amazed me.

"Well, first off, I saw you going that way 'long about ten o'clock when I climbed back up the ladder. And then later on, after all that excitement had died down, with you hauled away in the ambulance, I took me a walk through the meadow and found this." He pulled my camera out of his pocket, the camera I'd totally forgotten about. "I found it in the ditch."

"My birthday pictures," Teresa said, "are in that camera."

Bud said, "The sheriff asked me this morning if I knew about anything, but my memory doesn't always function, you know?" He put the camera into the bedside table drawer.

"Is the sheriff out to make an arrest?" I asked nervously.

"Aw, I think he's just doin' a normal investigation. Nothing bad happened except those tombstones gettin' switched around and that's no big deal. The sheriff told me himself that the little girl most likely did it, out of pure orneriness. But she's gone so there's nothing he can do about that."

"He's blaming Flora?"

"Well, he called her Sarah Elizabeth, but likely it's the same one. Said he'd suspected she was around, but no one ever spotted her. Said she'd never been anything but trouble."

I lunged for the phone.

"Jon, what are you doing?" Teresa asked sharply.

"I'm going to call the sheriff."

She grabbed the phone and moved it out of my reach. "You're not going to do any such stupid thing!"

"Yeah, Jon." Bud looked nervous. "Why would you want to do that?"

"I've got to explain how it was. I can't let Flora take all the blame."

"She's gone. So what does it matter?" my sister asked.

"It matters."

"Look." Teresa tried to take my hands but I snatched them away. "It's all very noble, your wanting to be the knight in shining armor, but it wouldn't do any good. And it could do lots of harm."

"Who to?"

"The folks."

"Why? They didn't even know about it."

"So what? You're their kid. We're all new here. And we're northerners! You get your name in the paper about this vandalism and see how fast people turn their backs on our parents! It could affect Dad's job." She leaned over the bed. "But all you care about is saving the rep of your little sweetheart!"

"She wasn't my sweetheart!" I shouted.

"All right, then. Your playmate. Anyway, I repeat. It won't help anyone if you step up and share the blame . . . and it can do lots of harm. Just think about it."

"Just leave," I told her.

She grabbed her purse and left.

I picked up the newspaper clipping. "Did you see this?" I asked Bud.

"Yeah. It struck me as kind of funny. All those dead bodies without their ID's." He sat on the chair near my bed. "Jon, I've got to tell you, you are the most interesting guy I have met in a long while. And it's a pleasure to be your friend. I mean that."

"Thanks, Bud. But I have to tell *you* something. I'm not all that interesting. This stuff just happened to me."

"But you took up with it and went along. Most guys wouldn't. Jon, I would purely love to see that trapdoor you've got in your closet someday."

"No problem. Come over as soon as they let me out of this firetrap. That may be tomorrow."

"I'll be there," Bud said.

♦

I spent a restless night. My parents had been at the hospital all evening. They tried to appear cheerful, but Dad looked worn out and Mom's eyes were swollen. I'd been nothing but worry for them all those weeks because of my extended sickness. Did I have the right to bring more trouble, of a different kind, to them now? Cause people to talk about them?

What should I do? Just keep quiet and let it all blow over, as Teresa had said?

And let Flora take all the blame. She wasn't ornery and she hadn't messed around with the tombstones just to cause trouble. She'd believed in what she was doing. And she believed in me. She trusted me. She and Kat had both trusted me.

I didn't know what to do. I honestly didn't.

In the morning the doctor said I could go home but only on the condition that I stay in bed for a solid week.

"Great," said Teresa, who'd come along with Mom to drive me home. "We get to wait on him all over again. Maybe I'll go down that ladder and break a leg, and then everyone can coo over me for a change."

"Ladder?" Mom asked. "What ladder?" So far she

and Dad had carefully avoided quizzing me about that night.

Teresa rolled her eyes. "Fasten your seat belt, as they say, Mom. It's quite a story."

"I'll tell you all about it," I said, leaving the hospital room with them. "When I've gained back my strength."

"Oh, please," said my sister.

TWENTY-TWO

♦ ♦ ♦

*D*ad came home for lunch that day to see how I was doing.

Making sure both my sisters were out of hearing, I told my parents what had been going on in my life. They were quite startled, as I'd suspected they might be.

"So what should I do?" I ended up. "I don't want to spoil things here for the two of you . . . but Flora shouldn't have to . . ."

"Don't worry about us," Dad said. "You do what is right."

"But what is right? Tell me!"

"Jon, you know," Mom said. It almost killed me to see her smile despite the tired look in her eyes.

"I guess I shouldn't have sneaked around . . . but it would've spoiled it all, to tell you two," I said. "Anyway, would you have let me do it if you'd known?"

"Not all you did. Not with your sickness," Dad said.

"Anyway, it's over," I said.

"Not quite over." Dad handed me the phone.

"Wh . . . what?"

"Make the call," he said. "It's okay. Really."

Mom kissed me and they left the room.

◆

Mrs. Tennyson showed the sheriff up to my room just a little while later. "Jon," she said, "this here's my cousin once removed, Sheriff Luther Davis. His bark's worse than his bite."

She turned to go, saying to the sheriff, "Now you be gentle with this boy, y'hear? He's been sick as can be, so don't you go bullying him around."

"I left my clubs and handcuffs out in the car, Willa Mae," he said. "Whyn't you go out and fetch them for me?" He laughed as his cousin gave a *humph!* and left.

The sheriff pulled up a chair next to my bed. "Now, you said you had something to tell me about night before last," he said. "What exactly would that be?"

He turned at the sound of a cough in the doorway. "Oh, Bud. Whyn't you just come on in? You a friend of Jon's here?"

"Yes, sir, I sure am. And I have something to add to what he's about to tell you."

"Well, now, you'd better pull up a chair. Maybe I can get the whole story all at once. I'd like that. You begin, Jon."

I repeated my story. Bud listened as raptly as he had the first time. His eyes kept shifting to my closet and I knew he was dying to see that secret passage, but he didn't get up.

When I'd finished talking, the sheriff sat there for a minute rubbing his chin with his hand. He finally cleared his throat and said, "Seems to me that it wasn't so much malicious mischief that was done. More like unjudicious actions. Know what I mean?"

"No, sir, I don't," I said.

"It's a matter of *intention*. Now, you didn't *intend* to do any harm, did you?"

I shook my head no.

"So I'd say you acted unwisely. Now, that's not exactly commendable, but still it's no crime."

"You got that right," Bud said. "Jon didn't mean any harm."

The sheriff kept looking at me. "Not a crime," he repeated, "but you did cause some inconvenience. So I'm going to have to ask you to make amends."

My heart sank. *How many years behind bars?* Or was he talking a big stiff fine?

"It's not right for those tombstones to be in the wrong places. So I'm going to leave it up to you to get them back where they belong."

"Sure," I said. "But . . . but how will I know?"

"Those graves are all documented. When you're up and feeling fit you can get a copy of the records and then go fix them."

"I'll help," Bud said.

The sheriff turned to him. "What is it you were going to add to this story?"

Bud explained about being on the ladder, painting, and seeing me, and then going to the meadow and hiding the pieces of the cement circle. "Does that make me an accessory after the fact?" he asked the sheriff.

The sheriff shook his head. "What do you kids do, watch every crime show on TV? Just go along and help your friend, Bud. And no more crime sprees in the graveyard. I got all I can do to ride herd on the living."

"Sheriff . . . one other thing . . ." Bud said.

The sheriff paused on his way to the door.

"My lips are goin' to be sealed about all this," Bud said, "because it would sure embarrass Jon to have all the kids in town findin' out about it."

"So what's your point?" the sheriff asked.

"I purely hope you will do all you can do to keep it out of the paper."

"All right," the sheriff said. "On one condition. I want you to promise me you won't make a career of painting houses like that one across the street."

Bud laughed. "Isn't that some sight?"

"The judges who gave them Stoneworths first prize ought to have their eyesight tested," Sheriff Davis said. "I just hope it doesn't start a trend in this town. Well," he said at the door, "I got to go out and catch me some real crooks. You boys are just small potatoes. See that you stay that way."

Mrs. Tennyson had been hovering outside the room. We heard her say to the sheriff as they started down the stairs, "Now, Luther, I want you to let this all blow over, y'hear?"

"Yes, ma'am," he said.

As soon as they'd gone, Bud leaped from his chair. "Now I can see that secret passage!" He raced to my closet and shuffled to the end of it. He called out, "I'm goin' all the way down and then back up!"

"I'll be here," I said.

That was the last time anyone used the passage. My dad had the trap doors nailed shut. "It's not safe," he said. "Imagine Colleen and her friends using it." That was more than *I* cared to imagine.

◆

One day, when my week of bed rest was almost over, Mom came to my room and said there was someone downstairs to see me. Wondering who it could be, I went down. Aunt Evangeline!

"I have a note," she said. "Flora made me promise to hand it to no one but you."

Shaking, I opened it. The handwriting was delicate, like Flora herself.

> *Dear Jon:*
> *It breaks my heart with sadness that I will not see you again soon. You are my really truly friend who believed in me. If I ever go to Katmandu I will find a new mountain, and when I do I will name it after you.*
> *Flora*

"Do you think she will ever come back?" I asked.

"No," the aunt said.

"Do you think her father will find her?"

"Perhaps. I want my sister to work things out. To get a new agreement. It would be for the best." She turned to the door. "I'll be leaving here soon myself. Good-bye, Jon. And thank you for helping Flora with her little midsummer night's dream. It meant a lot to her. Farewell."

"Farewell," I murmured, watching her go down the front steps. So I would never see Flora or Kat again. I bit my lip. I would not let tears come.

◆

It wasn't that night, but the night after, that I heard it. A faint meow out on the roof.

Was I imagining it? But then came a scratching on the screen, and I leaped out of bed. It was Kat. Flora's beloved odd eyed cat. I couldn't believe she hadn't taken him with her.

"Oh, Kat, Kat . . ." I snuggled him against me. "Where have you been? Has everyone gone now . . . and left you behind?"

As I rubbed my face against his neck I felt something rough. It was a paper, tied by ribbon around his neck. With shaky hands I unknotted the ribbon and read the note. It was in Flora's handwriting.

I am yours now, but remember, you do not possess me.

Kat

"You've been waiting for Flora, haven't you?" I asked. "But she's gone, kitty," I said. "Gone. Maybe forever."

Now I could accept that.

♦

As the months go by, Flora has become almost a fantasy . . . something soft and drifting from my summer of sickness.

Sometimes I dream I see her dancing in the meadow, her hair shimmery with moonbeams. But when I reach out to touch her, she's transparent . . . she's only an illusion.

I promised myself I would keep Flora forever in my mind, as surely she has kept me in hers. I would always remember those brief nights when for a while make-believe things were real.

Yet, I must confess that, caught up in school and sports and friends, I sometimes go through stretches of forgetting all about Flora. And then Kat, sensing my abandonment, goes away.

But when he returns and scratches on my window, I rush to let him in. And then, my face buried in his fur, I remember once again how it was last summer. I remember Flora. I remember the scent of flowers.